AGENT OF HORROR

AGENT OF HORROR

THE HUNT FOR THE NEXT BIG SCARE

C.J. LAWSON

Website:
cj-lawson.mailchimpsites.com

For information contact: coltonlawson44@gmail.com

Published by: Purplest Premier Publishing

The story, all names, characters, and incidents portrayed in this production
are fictitious. No identification with actual persons (living or deceased),
places, buildings, and products is intended or should be inferred.

Cover and interior book design
by Francine Eden Platt • Eden Graphics
Cover illustration of figure: Augusto de Silva @_.augustosilva._
partially created by MidJourney
Stock images on cover: iStockphoto: Kuromily, Jobalou
DepositPhotos: pikisuperstar
Stock images interior: iStockphoto: Marina Dekhnik;

Paperback ISBN 979-8-89454-066-5

eBook ISBN 979-8-89454-067-2

Audiobook ISBN 979-8-89454-068-9

Library of Congress Control Number:
2025909161

Manufactured in the United States of America
First Edition

DEDICATION

To the wonderful students, faculty, volunteers, and missionaries of Salt Lake Valley Institute which I was privileged to help with for a time. While this applies to everyone regardless of their role in the institute, I wanted to give special permission to the students to tell people that yes, there is a book dedicated to you.

Dear Reader,

THANK YOU for picking up this book. Along with its author, we are very happy that you did. While it's true that the story has its main characters, the narrator got a little unruly at times and just couldn't keep things to himself. He made his comments quite clear and was adamant that they stay on the pages. When you see them, just smile and let him have his moment. One day he hopes to be a main character in a book himself, *but that day is not today.*

ACKNOWLEDGMENTS

FOR SEVERAL YEARS, as recovering edgy teenagers, Eddie Cazier and I would meet in our weekly Avant-garde Creationist meetings (it's a writer's club, not a cult). We'd discuss our serious and dramatic books. The ones we hoped would change the world. It was in one of these meetings that I first vocalized the strange idea of a man with a top hat looking for the next "big scare."

Had he said it was a "stupid" idea, this book probably would not be in your hands now, and the paper it is printed on would likely be used in a dictionary or something far more useful. I am truly grateful for Eddie, my lifelong friend. Not only did he like the idea, but when I repeatedly said I did not want to do any humorous writing besides an occasional unpublished short story here and there, it was Eddie who suggested there could be something more. I owe him thanks in all of my projects. (Sorry Eddie, you're going to be in every single acknowledgements page of mine.) But in this one you deserve special attention. So, thank you, my friend.

Similarly, with all of my projects, I want to acknowledge my loving and supporting family. My mother and brother have never patronized my dreams, suggesting I pick a more stable profession, even though they probably should. It's moments like this where I most miss my father, whom I'm sure would have loved this story, but I know it was thanks to his 'unique' blend of humor that I now write this. I'm sure there are books in heaven though, so maybe he'll get a laugh out of it; and if there aren't books in heaven, is it really heaven?

I also want to thank my Author Ready friends, especially Debbie's weekly reading group who have continually encouraged this more experimental type of writing. It's published now Stan; you can stop asking about it.

There are many others I can't thank by name either because of the incredible people you are or because of the way your fears inspired something in the book. You can choose which category you fall into. Regardless, thank you.

TABLE OF CONTENTS

Horace Blackwater Back in Action

So, IT WAS A DARK AND STORMY NIGHT, but to Horace Blackwater, that was just about as normal as a bright and sunny day. It wasn't because he had some weird power over the weather, don't get me wrong—that would be cool. But Horace was an agent of horror. All year round, his business was to deal with the spooky and sinister. An agent of horror's primary responsibility was to "find" scary things and bring them into the limelight. However, anything that fit nicely in spooky culture worked just as well.

Many take for granted all the work an agent of horror does, but if not for them, no one would've ever heard of Dracula or Frankenstein. When Horace was still in training, he helped discover the headless horseman, and in his prime, Horace invented the tablecloth ghost costume. For a while, he even received a check with twenty-five cents every time someone wore the costume; let's just say there have been some complications with the IRS.

But that was a long story. He was already in retirement when the unfortunate incident occurred, and it somehow forced him all the way to Romania, into a second, less desirable retirement.

Back to the dark and stormy night.

Horace would have taken a ride-share service, but that was too scary even for him. So instead, wearing his thick dark boots, he walked through mud up a winding pathway. His black coat loosely shielded him from the light drizzle. His top hat served a similar purpose. A small white pin was attached to the collar of his jacket. It was of a tablecloth ghost, but this particular pin was made by his daughter when she was in elementary school. Now she was an adult doing who knows what, but Horace had seldom removed the pin in all those years, and he kept a hand clutched over it now to protect it from the rain.

Only a madman would make such a journey on foot in these conditions. Well, he *was* mad, despite that, he had a good reason for such a journey. His home was being cleaned, so he had worked out a deal to stay at an old friend's house while the process was being done. This friend *lived* in Romania, in the region of Transylvania. He was the famous… *(and officially public domain)* …Count Dracula.

As Horace neared the mansion, he grinned, reveling in the Gothic style and imposing nature of the building. The heavy rain added to the atmosphere, and a bolt of lightning in the distance caused a flash of inspiration in Horace's mind.

It wasn't scary to him, but he imagined a group of delinquents coming across it late at night and daring each other to step ever closer to the mansion. But then, something horrendous would come out, chase them around, and eat them all up one by one. Because, apparently, that's what went on in the mind of an agent of horror.

Well, an *ex*-agent of horror.

Horace lamented the lost days of his youth as the twelve steps to the door took more energy out of him than he was willing to admit. When he reached the door, he took a moment to catch his breath.

"Hi!" announced a happy and chipper electronic voice. "You are now being recorded."

The voice came from a camera next to the door. Everything about the house—the large wooden door, the expansive walls and windows, and further back the spiked gates—all matched the Gothic presence of the owner's personality.

That camera sticks out like a clown at a funeral.

Horace glanced at five boxes stacked as tall as him next to the door. "I'm not here to steal your packages," Horace said with a grin as he prodded them, surprised at their weight.

Just what did he order, anyway?

It would have to be answered later because, while he was curious, he wasn't about to open them in front of a camera. Horace pressed the doorbell; immediately disappointed by the lack of a spooky jingle. The sound was the most generic trademark-free doorbell sound imaginable.

"What was that?" A feminine voice came through the same speaker as the electronic, although this was clearly not the same one.

"Sister, the camera's not working. I can't see who's there." A different young feminine voice.

"Try pressing all the buttons."

"What do you think I did?"

"Sisters." This time, a deeper, more authoritative feminine voice. "Assume the worst. Flush the evidence while we still have a chance."

"Yes, sister," the first two responded in unison.

It sounded to Horace like they were running around frantically. It had not yet occurred to him that this might be a two-way microphone.

"It's not flushing," a voice cried out.

"Flush harder," cried another.

"We've got to burn it. It's not working."

"But how, sister?"

"Pour some oil on it and start a blaze."

"I'm not…" Horace hoped they could hear him. But he guessed, that even if the speaker was two-way, it wouldn't matter, anyway.

"Oh, really, sister? Let me just open up the oil drawer that I keep downstairs."

"I thought you used it as eyeliner sometimes."

"I know there's some vegetable oil in the kitchen."

Silence.

Maybe I should come back another time before I'm accused of arson.

"Sister, you're a genius."

Horace considered pressing the doorbell again, but he couldn't be sure if that would excite the females even more and cause them to dowse the entire building.

"Hey," through the speaker, another voice echoed.

Horace knew this one.

"Could one of you get the door? I'm pretty sure it's Horace." It was Dracula, but he wasn't speaking in his stage accent

(Unfortunately, many famous monsters and ghouls typically speak in a standard American accent and not the fun, imaginative, and probably culturally insensitive voices most people imagined).

"Why don't *you* get the door for once," one of the younger voices snapped back.

"Wait...sisters," said the female voice of authority. "Maybe our days are finally numbered. I don't think any amount of vegetable oil will save us. Let's accept our fate with dignity."

"Yes, sister," the two answered together.

"Horace told me he was coming by tonight..." said Dracula, but much like Horace's voice, it fell on deaf ears of the sisters.

After a series of clicks, the door unlocked. Horace

strained to hear frantic whispers from the other side. At long last, it opened, revealing a tall, ghostly pale woman with blonde hair.

Her face noticeably relaxed, and Horace nodded curtly.

"Oh, I'm so glad you're not the police."

Ahhh, the authoritative voice.

Two much younger but equally pale girls poked their heads around the door. Horace assumed they were the other two he had heard.

"Horace, come on in." Dracula's voice boomed from somewhere above.

The journey had been long and physically challenging for Horace, and evidently, it had been an emotional roller coaster for the sisters. The spacious mansion was just as Horace remembered.

Dracula descended the grand staircase, the main attraction in the center of the room.

"Did the speakers work?" asked one of the sisters.

"Does the camera?" asked the other sister.

"Oh, I don't know about the camera, but the speakers worked great," Horace said to the sisters.

"It comes with speakers too?" said one of the girls.

"I told you it was a good purchase," said the other as they walked away and disappeared into one of the many rooms.

I guess introductions will be made later…

Dracula finally made it down the stairs. "Horace!"

As he moved closer, it was apparent Dracula was going

in for a bro hug. Horace reluctantly accepted; although, he instinctively moved his head, his neck more specifically, away from Dracula's head during the embrace. It was, thankfully, unnoticed by the vampire.

"It's been too long," said Dracula, still hugging Horace. For good measure, he patted Horace's back twice.

Horace was so ready for this to be over, but it continued for a few more uncomfortable seconds.

Dracula finally pulled away. "You look great."

"Thank you," Horace said. "You don't look like you've aged a day since I last saw you."

"May I take your coat, Mr. Blackwater?" the stern woman asked.

Before Horace could answer, Dracula said, "Oh, please, this is Horace. He's the one who helped me really take off. I don't know anyone who calls him Mr. Blackwater."

"Well… *Mr.* Horace, can I take your coat then?" she corrected, although Horace slightly resented the "mister" talk.

You're no spring chicken either lady.

He held one hand in front of him. "No, that's fine. I feel naked without it."

"Well, it's late," said Dracula. "Why don't I show you to your room, and we can talk in the morning."

"That would be splendid." Horace turned to the woman. "*Madam*," he bid adieu then followed Dracula up the stairs and down a long hallway.

"My home is your home, Horace," he said, "But it's

kind of a safety hazard if you fall asleep in any other room besides your bedroom."

"I won't ask for details."

Dracula laughed.

Unable to contain his curiosity, Horace asked, "Speaking of safety hazards, what's in all those boxes out front?"

"Oh, it's here? I don't always get the emails. It's soil from Napa Valley."

"You ordered dirt online?"

"Yes, for my garden."

"Drac, I marched through a mile of mud, and you ordered some dirt from halfway around the world. Dirt is the one thing you can take for free from anywhere. It's dirt, for crying out loud."

"Yes, but it doesn't grow on trees now, does it?" Dracula brought up one finger in defense.

It was a feeble protest—one Horace would have crushed in an instant if he had the chance —but just then, they arrived at Horace's room.

"And here we are." Dracula smiled. He seemed happy to change the subject away from his dirt purchasing habits. "Call if you need anything."

"I ought to be fine." Horace opened the door. This room was much more luxurious than his entire cottage, and about the same size too.

"Oh," Dracula called from the hallway, "and Terra should be here sometime tomorrow afternoon."

Horace froze. "Terra?"

"Yep."

"What in blazes is Terra doing here?"

"Well, she's not here yet."

Horace could feel his blood pressure rising.

"I thought you knew. Didn't you plan to visit here together?"

"No—I..."

"Maybe she wanted to surprise you." Dracula chuckled. "Well... uh... I'll be on my way. I've packages to open."

And just like that, the vampire hurried on his way out of this increasingly uncomfortable conversation, leaving Horace dumbfounded.

What does she want with me, anyway? She should be off pursuing her own life.

He shook his head and gently closed the door. The click ushered in another layer of silence, allowing his mind to wander to all the possibilities.

She was so eager to go off to college. Her life is blooming—she doesn't need me. No one needs a relic like me anymore. That's why I'm an ex-agent of horror.

Horace patted the pillow on his bed, making sure it was soft enough for his liking.

He had decided that Terra would be wasting her time by coming here. As her father, there was nothing he could give her he hadn't already, and there had been no contact between them since he moved to Romania. There was no reason to be. Her life was just beginning, and his was winding to a close.

She would lead a happier life without me dragging her down.

Lying there in bed, the thought tumbled over and over in his mind.

Horace tossed and turned all night, wondering what he should say to Terra, and what she would say to him. She had always been independent, but women were confusing, and now Horace worried she would be upset with him for leaving her alone for so long, or some other reason he hadn't yet foreseen. Occasionally, he wondered about the dirt Dracula had been ordering online.

Just how much can you make by selling dirt?

A knock on the door caused him to finally get up. The morning light was shining through the window beside his bed. The storm continued as if bound by a legal contract to always rain at this mansion.

"Mr. Blackwater?" a voice called out. "Breakfast is served in the dining room."

Horace opened the door to one of the pale sisters. This one was probably a few years younger than Terra. He still didn't know her name, and at this point, it seemed awkward to ask her for it.

Maybe Dracula introduced us before.

Putting his pride above his courtesy, he decided that, until he learned otherwise, he would call this woman Unoone. He patted himself on the back for his elementary level understanding of Spanish, and his creativity, which was comparable to a child with duct tape.

"The Count sent me to wake you," said Uno-one.

Nodding, Horace said, "Yes, thank you." When she didn't leave, he knew what would come next. He'd seen it many times.

"Uh, Mr. Blackwater?"

"Horace."

"Mr. Horace, I was wondering if you have any advice. I'd like to break into the horror business someday, and I…"

"Well, I'm retired," said Horace.

The two started down the hall.

"Yes, but the Count says you were the best in the business for spotting new potential."

Horace nodded, padding his ego as they neared the stairs. They descended each step slowly and deliberately.

"Unfortunately, that was a long time ago," said Horace. "I never could understand the younger generation. They have a different mindset. The same horror tricks don't work anymore."

"Yes, but…"

"You know, when we first invented film, all we had to do was cut out bats and attach them to fishing poles. That was enough to have people scared silly. Or a train coming down a track at the camera had people falling over each other to escape the theatre. Now, a serial killer with a chainsaw is boring, but the Teletubbies are terrifying, and Winnie the Pooh is downright traumatic. There's no logic from what I can see in the modern trends."

Uno-one nodded in agreement with him.

They arrived at the dining room where Dracula sat at the end of a long table. The other girl and the woman were setting out the dishes. He had determined the other younger sisters would be called Dos-two. And the old woman would naturally have another name fitting with the pattern: Ruth.

Horace made some unique patterns—sometimes.

"So, we should try to market to children? Is that the key to being scary?" asked Uno-one.

"No, I don't think that's it," said Horace.

"Oh, we could make educational videos," Dos-two chimed in. "There's nothing children find scarier than education."

Horace thought for a moment. He had heard some really bad ideas in his time. Some were so dumb that no matter how hard he tried to forget them, they'd reappear in his deepest, darkest nightmares. This was not one of those ideas; it had potential. It needed a lot of work, but a passive-aggressive, somewhat scary series of educational material just might hit it big. Perhaps, even in this modern age.

But Horace brushed aside his thoughts. He was no longer an agent of horror. His time of grooming and improving ideas was behind him. He would probably make it worse if he tried. Yet, still like a bird yearning to fly, or a child blowing into a whistle the second they get it, Horace yearned to create something new, and no matter how much he tried to silence that voice, it kept coming back.

Uno-one turned to Dracula. "Do you think we can give it a try?"

"Of course," he said.

Horace took his seat opposite the Count, removed his hat, and placed it beside his plate. His hair was straggly and gray, but it was a good healthy shade. At least Horace had told himself it was.

The sisters had laid out a continental breakfast that looked homemade, but Horace noticed the wrappers at the top of the trash can. Nonetheless, he was grateful. He took his fork and knife and began cutting into a pastry that he guessed had an unpronounceable name.

"So, Horace, how's retirement?" asked Dracula.

"What do you do anyway now that you're retired?" Ruth sipped her coffee.

Wait to die…

Horace wanted to answer, but he didn't. "I haven't really found anything. I did have a nice place in the States, but I moved here a little while ago and haven't been able to do much."

It was a depressing answer and even Horace knew that, but it was better than what he first thought. "Although," he added, hoping to resurrect the conversation. "I might take up gardening. If I do, I think I'll use the soil at my home instead of ordering abroad."

A confusion settled over the women, and Dracula shrugged, then changed the subject. "So, what's Terra been up to?"

He really doesn't like talking about the dirt… Sounds like I have some dirt on him should the need ever arise.

"Well…" began Horace. "She was eager to go to university once she graduated from high school. So, she left right away."

"What was she studying?" asked Uno-one.

"Something…academic as I recall."

Dos-two asked, "Is she all finished then?"

"Well, she's been there for three, or is it four years?"

"I'm sure she would have invited you to the graduation," said Dracula.

"Yes, but I don't think she has my new address."

Uno-one shrugged. "Couldn't she text you?"

"No." The more they talked about Terra, the more Horace realized that this might be a truly scary reunion.

What would they even talk about when she did arrive?

He reached into his coat's deep pockets and produced his wallet. He at least had pictures of her in there. The one at the top was his favorite. It was the two of them on her fourteenth Halloween. She was going through a goth phase at the time, much to Horace's delight. She had an even paler face than the sisters, and her naturally brown hair was dyed jet black. There was also a patch of blood red in her hair, and she wore a leather necklace with spikes on it. But, as she put it, she had long since gotten her life together and ditched the goth and the dyes.

Horace heard one of the sisters say, "So, she's been to college and survived."

"There are so many things I can't wait to ask her," another added.

Horace took a deep, anxious breath as he stared at her picture.

They grow up way too fast.

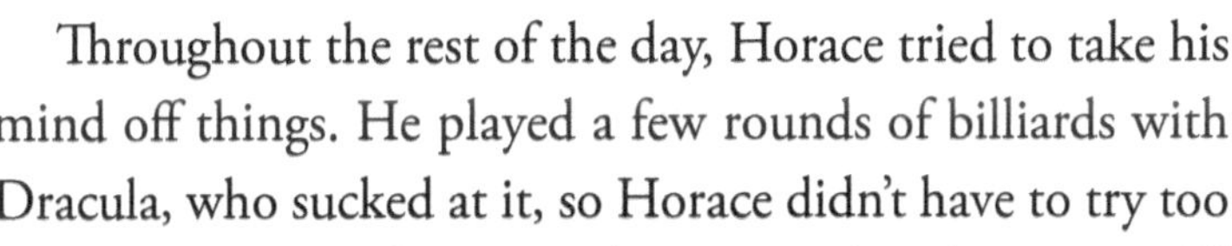

Throughout the rest of the day, Horace tried to take his mind off things. He played a few rounds of billiards with Dracula, who sucked at it, so Horace didn't have to try too hard, and his mind remained tormented with anxiety. All the while, Dracula pouted about being unable to win a single game.

The generic ringing through the house reminded Horace that he had not yet ridiculed the Count for his lack of flair in his doorbell. Then he remembered his much more urgent concern and took a deep breath to ready himself.

Dracula donned his most cliché black and red cape before the two hurried up the stairs.

Ruth had already answered the door and was talking to Terra.

His daughter had grown somewhat since he had last seen her. She was slightly taller than him, and her hair had some dark highlights, but nothing that was goth. She had a light brown overcoat which Ruth was taking when Horace walked in. The lighter shade of the coat made Horace wonder if it was a small act of defiance against him, but the rest of her attire was dark, so he couldn't be sure. She wore a dark blue blouse with long sleeves and loose artsy-looking pants. Much to his surprise, her eyes lit up with joy when she saw him.

"Dad!"

"Ah, hello, Terra," Dracula spoke in his Transylvanian accent.

No one ever wanted to tell him it was bad, and if you think about it, Dracula doing a bad Dracula accent didn't quite make sense, but his accent was atrocious.

The "hello" sounded more like "yellow."

"I remember you when you were yay tall." He held his hand an inch above the floor. "It's so good to see you again, my dear."

Dracula moved a little closer, and the two hugged.

Back off Drac, she's nineteen… no wait, she's twenty. She might be twenty-one now that I think about it.

Once Dracula's uninvited interruption was over, the reunion was allowed to continue.

"Dad." Terra moved away from the Count and threw her arms around her father.

Horace returned the gesture and felt his fears fading away. Ordinarily, that would be bad for an agent of horror, even an ex-agent of horror, but it wasn't worth ruining the moment over.

"I was so worried after you disappeared," said Terra.

"Oh, you shouldn't worry. It wasn't much."

"Dad, you had to leave the country. I heard rumors the president was even involved."

"Ah, I'd rather put the whole incident behind me."

"Come, child," Dracula said, motioning toward the large undead room. (It was called the living room everywhere else).

"Dinner is a ways off, but you must tell us about your studies."

By now, Dracula's accent was fading. It was more Russian now than Vampire.

Horace rolled his eyes. "Drop the voice, Drac, she's family."

"Right," said Dracula in his normal voice. "You must be tired. Sit, relax."

The three of them took their seats on one of the large Victorian sofas that littered the room. The furniture pattern would give any interior designer a heart attack.

Ruth and the sisters returned to the kitchen to prepare dinner which involved some actual cooking, unlike breakfast.

Terra looked around the surroundings. "I think I remember being here a long time ago…"

"That's right," Horace said. "We were here a few times for parties and celebrations. Dracula and I go way back."

"I remember when you were yay high," Dracula said again and returned to his gruff Stalin-like accent.

"Yes, she remembers," Horace interjected.

"Have you been okay, Dad?" Terra asked. "The rumors from that incident were wild. It sounded like you could face some serious jail time."

Horace waved his hand. "Ah, it's nothing I couldn't handle. Just a bit of bad luck with the IRS, and now I'm relocated. They took everything I owned, so they're satisfied with how it turned out. It's nothing I thought to worry you about."

"But once everything had passed, you didn't even think to leave a note or try to call me. I was worried sick."

And there it was. Horace knew this was likely the reason for her visit.

"I didn't want it to distract you. You're just starting your life, and you have so many happy days ahead of you. Drac and I are relics of a bygone day. There's not much for us to look forward to. I remember how eager I was to start my work as an agent of horror, and I assumed you were eager to start your own career with whatever you decided. You didn't need to know about my problems. They'd just distract you, dear."

Terra slumped, and Horace noticed her eyes soften the way they always did before she cried.

"Wow, that's really depressing, Horace," said Drac. It was as though he had not read the room whatsoever. Then he added, "You make it sound like she didn't care about you."

"B…but I did care about you. I *do* care about what happens to you," said Terra.

"I never said that. I just said that you didn't need to worry about your old man."

"I don't see the difference…"

"Shut it, Drac," said Horace.

Ruth walked abruptly in on the conversation. "Dinner is ready."

"Speaking of things *I* care about." Dracula was the first to rise. The Blackwaters quickly followed, and they found the table was set similar to how it was this morning with an additional seat for Terra, next to her father.

On his other side was Dos-two, who won a rock paper scissors best of seven tournament.

"I don't think we've been introduced," said Ruth, nodding toward Terra.

She smiled. "No, I don't think so."

Dracula grimaced, rubbing his face as Uno-one and Dos-two reached under the table. One retrieved a kazoo and the other a recorder.

"They've insisted that they can only give their names through a cheesy song," Dracula explained.

Horace could feel his heart rate quicken. This was going to be a long painful song, the kind that halted the plot for five minutes just to give the most basic information.

I'm not about to subject myself and my daughter to fifth-rate Broadway!

Horace jumped up just as the first note from the recorder sounded. "That's Uno-one, that's Dos-two and that's Ruth," he pointed to each one as he spoke.

"B-but that's not my name," said Uno-one.

"A-and the song-" said Dos-two.

"Too bad," Horace said, folding his arms.

Terra was so happy she had finally found her dad. Once she graduated, all of her time was devoted to tracking him down. It was easier than she would have thought, but still it had taken several months, and now it felt strange to be having dinner with him again.

She looked around the table. The dinner was beautiful; roast, potatoes, and garlic bread. Everything looked incredible and yet her eyes lingered questioningly on the garlic bread. Before she could comment on it, Horace beat her to it.

"Why the garlic bread?" asked Horace.

"We heard it's really good," said Ruth. "So, we wanted you to have some."

Dracula raised his eyebrows. "If I ever contract some incurable illness, I think I'd like to try it. Just once."

"It's not worth dying over. But pass some this way," said Terra with a smirk.

Uno-one asked Terra, "So, you've actually been to a university?"

"That's right." Terra took a bite of the coveted garlic bread. "This just might be worth dying for." The conversation had given her enough time to tell them that. She had finished college with an English degree and a minor in mythology. Her schooling had finished only a few months ago when she started looking for Horace.

"We've so many questions about the outside world," said Dos-two.

Terra anticipated their questions. What campus life was like, or how was it being on your own, or even since they looked to be about her age, she thought they might ask her about the boys found on campus, but she wasn't exactly comfortable talking about that in front of her father. Their questions, however, managed to exceed her expectation.

"Are birds real?"

"What?" Terra nearly choked on the heaven-sent garlic bread.

"We've heard about birds from the government, but we've never actually seen one," Dos-two explained.

"And we heard they gather where people are, so we thought you might have seen them while you were on campus," added Uno-one.

"Yes, I've seen many birds, but never a penguin," said Ruth.

"No. They don't live in the States," said Terra.

"I figured birds could be real, but penguins were too far-fetched," explained Ruth.

"Oh, Terra, have you ever seen a real ginger?"

"For the love of all that's good in horror, Drac, just how sheltered are these girls?" Horace shook his head.

Dracula shrugged. "Okay, to be fair, there aren't many gingers in Romania."

There was enough laughter from the women to drop the issue, but it was one more thing Horace knew he needed to have a long talk with Dracula about.

"So, aside from the Count, how many people did you recruit, Mr. Blackwater?" asked Dos-two.

"Well, it wasn't always people. Sometimes I'd 'recruit' animals or find new traditions that people could take up to celebrate the scary. The Count has probably told you about the tablecloth ghost costume I invented."

The sisters looked fascinated by his stories.

"I also helped a lot with making pumpkins as popular as they are now."

Terra watched her father as he reminisced. As a child, she had always remembered how happy her father was with his work.

She'd never told him, but she wanted to do the same thing when she grew up. Now was the perfect time to approach the subject she'd wanted to ask ever since she arrived. "Why did you stop, anyway?"

The clattering of silverware came to an abrupt silence, and everyone looked at Horace as if waiting for an answer. The sudden attention seemed to make him uncomfortable. "Like most things, I got old and outdated, I guess."

"Do you ever want to go back and try again?" asked Terra.

"All the time, but I made my fortune. Granted, the IRS took most of it, but I can survive for a while in my cottage, and if all else fails, I can move in with the Count."

Dracula's head shot up, but he didn't have time to say anything.

"What if I helped you?" Terra suggested.

"You?" Horace looked surprised.

"Yes. I've always been curious about it, and I think I could be useful. My English degree isn't good for much else beyond teaching, but it might help recognize the literary potential of scary things. Same with the mythology degree, I mean, I can't even teach it, so I'm not sure what I *can* use it for."

"Well…" A grin spread across Horace's face as a flood of ideas started to come to him. It was just like back in the good old days when he had a constant stream of ideas. Most of them were rubbish, but on occasion, he'd find a gem in the dirt pile. "You'd probably find it dreadfully boring."

"No, I wouldn't, I promise." Terra's eyes filled with tears.

"Come on, Horace," Dracula said in a light voice. "You know you want to."

It was true. Ever since the incident and even since he had retired, he'd wanted to get back in the game. There were some things that were undeniable. Artists are drawn to create art, birds (which *are* real) are drawn to fly, and agents of horror, like Horace, are drawn to the scary.

Horace's sinister grin made Terra smile. She recognized that look.

"Well then, shall we begin?" he asked.

The Wicking of Wax

HORACE AND TERRA had barely finished their dinner when they set out, but it was late, and the nearest place to stay was—well, at Dracula's castle, so they went back, spent the night, and then woke up at the crack of dawn.

The mud path Horace trekked through to arrive at the mansion was an alternate path to the more maintained route, that even had a sidewalk. For anyone else, it would have been a beautiful walk through nature, but for agents of horror, it was the perfect time to brainstorm.

"Where do we start?" Terra asked eagerly, ready to begin her career as an agent of horror, or at least, an assistant.

"Inspiration is a fickle thing, my dear," Horace said. "Most people understand the world as the three states of matter, but inspiration is like that fourth state. The nerd is always quick to point out it exists, but he seldom understands it."

She hadn't seen her father this eccentric in a long time. "So…do you know where we can find some…plasma?"

"Of course." Horace chuckled. "I've had a few years to

think, so we have many options available to us. There's a dying industry not too far from here that I've always thought had the potential to be very scary."

"What kind of industry?"

"Wax."

Terra waited for some grander reveal. "Candles? You think candles can be scary?" Maybe he was still in his slump, after all.

"Who said anything about candles? I'm talking about wax."

"But isn't wax used to make candles."

Horace dropped his shoulders and his eccentricity, for the moment. "Clearly, you don't understand. There's a wax museum not far from here."

"They make museums for wax?"

"It's not the wax that's special, but what the artists do with it. You'd be surprised how flesh-like wax can appear. These museums are like galleries with very realistic-looking people made from wax."

"Oh, that does sound kind of creepy."

"Precisely!" Horace pointed at his daughter in excitement. "Many readily recognize the creepiness of it. It's like human taxidermy only you don't need a corpse. These wax museums mainly focus on the rich and famous so that people can get selfies or whatever it is they do nowadays and then show them off to their friends as if they had actually met some talentless schmuck who's richer than they'll ever be."

"That does sound kind of cool, actually." Terra began imagining her favorite celebrities but made of wax. If it was just a photo, no one would know the difference.

"This particular wax museum has an interesting theme: insignificant moments and people from history," said Horace.

"Don't you think that might be kind of offensive?"

"It's irrelevant, really." Horace dismissed it with a wave of his hand. "The important thing is that they're breaking from the mold, so to speak, and may be willing to try more horror-themed wax abominations."

The walk to the wax museum was much shorter than anticipated. Horace was discouraged by the fact that not a soul was in line for entry.

As with the theme, there were a variety of wax sculptures and scenes depicted in the museum. Some of the most noteworthy included the man who planted the apple tree that Isaac Newton sat under when he discovered gravity, the first person arrested for jaywalking (depicted in chains, although, they appear to be ready at any moment to break their chains with the amount of anger they held), the last senator to stab Julius Caesar, and the grand centerpiece of the museum for the month: President Taft in the bathtub. A layer of plastic soap covered most of the tub and President Taft's private parts. A plaque in front of it explained the whole ordeal of how Taft was once stuck in the White House's bathtub, and how they ended up using butter to save the larger-than-life president. It also noted how there was technically *no evidence* of the event.

"Presidents often have the power to remove evidence which incriminates them," Horace commented.

"What about Nixon?"

Horace ignored the comment because he didn't have a clever comeback, and he refused to admit that he was wrong.

"I haven't seen a single employee since the front desk." Horace noted as they continued to tour the works.

"That is kind of strange," Terra said finally, seemingly to finally be aware of the quietness.

Horace wondered if she noticed the creepiness of the situation, but he didn't ask.

He inched closer to a wax depiction of Louis XIX

(19, I can't read Roman numerals either).

The plague before him described how technically he was the King of France for twenty minutes, in other words, less time than Taft was stuck in the tub.

"These are pretty unnerving. Do you think we could find a sculptor and make him famous, or are you thinking of a specific wax creation?" asked Terra.

"Neither is a bad idea, but I was thinking of reinventing wax sculpting altogether." Horace rubbed his chin. "You see, when you mentioned candles earlier, I had a brilliant idea."

"What's that?" asked Terra, eagerly.

"Candles run off wax, not to be too technical—but if

we were to stick a wick into a wax sculpture, it would slowly melt in a horrific abomination. Like a snowman slowly melting but surely becoming more and more deformed beyond what any human artist could ever create."

Terra shivered. "This *is* creepy."

"I think the eyes would make for a great place to store the flames. That way, the face gets the most deformed. We could run the rope into every part of the body so it all melts equally."

"That might be pushing it just…" Terra attempted to interject, but Horace was in the mode now.

He rubbed his hands together and grinned. "And there could be a whole new facility created where people can send pictures of their loved ones, and wax sculptures can be made based off the pictures and then melt right before their eyes."

"Dad! That would be traumatizing!"

Horace chuckled a little. "What's trauma if not a sign of success in our field?"

"Dad!" Terra rolled her eyes and shook her head.

Horace stopped. Suddenly, his thoughts jumped to thinking about the ramifications of such an event. "Well, I suppose that might be going a little too far. Either way, we'll need to find the sculptor of these wax figurines. Let's split up and cover more ground."

Before Terra could offer a rebuttal, Horace marched away down a hallway labeled, "First Discoveries that you wouldn't want on your Resume." His disappearance was so quick that Terra couldn't help but wonder if there was another reason for it.

Maybe it was her.

She was eager to help her father get back into the business, but maybe she was causing more harm than good.

Terra knew she was there for a reason. Her father had the talent to recognize greatness, he'd done so quite successfully for years, but she thought of herself as the bridge for him into this new century, and the first thing she did was to tell him how horrible of an idea it would be. It was the kind of argument where no one—everyone was to blame. If this father/daughter duo was going to work, she knew she'd have to earn his respect, only she didn't know how.

The more Terra thought about it, the more she convinced herself she was the problem, as was the way with young people. She regretted every word she'd spoken to him ever since they first reunited. All she wanted to do was spend time with him and learn the trade he'd spent years building.

It didn't help that the section of the museum she was in, "Useless Politicians who Failed even by Politician's Standards," was filled with wax figures she was quite sure were all judging her. Some had long pointed noses, others regular short ones, and one even had no nose at all. But all of their eyes looked so alive and so judgmental. It reminded her of stereotypical in-laws. They ask what their children were planning to do with their lives, and even when they were given a good answer, the in-laws would find a way to belittle the profession or choice.

"Sounds like a pyramid scheme."

Did I just hear that?

She turned to one of the wax men and stared into his eyes. Out of curiosity, she read his plaque. He was a politician who ran as a candidate in over a hundred races but won only once—a school board member, but it later came out that he had stuffed ballots.

She held her head up, jutted her chin out, and scoffed at the wax man. She left the political nightmare and tried to find more friendly wax figurines. However, no matter where she went, they all looked upset. Maybe at themselves or maybe at others.

This is a museum of failures. Maybe I should just find a place to stand for eternity since I'm going to be joining them, anyway. What difference does it make if it's in wax or flesh?

Terra, who was doing quite a good job of beating herself up, wasn't done yet. "I'll never be an agent of horror," she whimpered. "My dad was the best in the business, but I'll be the worst if I even make it that far…"

She passed through a hallway of failed inventors where she saw a bench in the middle of a large room. Horace was sitting on the edge in a sort of thinking pose. She cursed herself for voicing her doubts when her father was just around the corner, but it appeared he hadn't heard her.

Terra slumped onto the bench beside him, but he didn't move. "How'd it go with the wax sculptor?" Sadness dripped with every syllable.

When there was no answer, Terra continued, "That good, huh?"

Horace was silent and still, just like the wax figurines.

"I'm sorry I dragged you out of retirement…" Terra tried to start a serious conversation with the motionless Horace.

Her dad didn't say anything, so she continued.

"I…I never told you, but I always wanted to follow in your footsteps… I know we talked when I left for college that I was finally going to take my own path in life, but I still wanted you to be a part of it."

Horace was so good at imitating the wax sculptures that he did not even blink. He didn't even breath, and yet his skin remained the same color.

"I didn't mean to make you upset. I know I'm no good at this, so maybe I should keep my mouth shut."

Speaking of mouths being shut, Horace's mouth was shut, and he remained as still as a statue.

"No," Terra said suddenly. "I…I can help you… You said so yourself. I have a different perspective on the world, so it's your fault for getting so upset at my suggestion." Terra started to cry, and she stopped talking. After a long pause, she continued, "No, I'm sorry, that's not what I meant."

All of the wax figures waited in silence, I mean, that's all they could do all the time, but somehow it seemed fitting here, and Horace, *exactly* like the wax sculptures, did the same.

"I know it's gonna be difficult and new, but I want to travel around with you and find new and exciting big scares. So, I know we had a bit of a rough start, but… if it's okay with you, I want to keep going."

Terra had been so invested in this conversation that she hadn't heard the footsteps slowly approaching.

"Terra," Horace's voice rang out loud and clear from behind her, despite the fact that Horace's mouth didn't move.

Startled, Terra jumped from the bench, spotting a second, much livelier Horace standing with a bag of chips in hand. She looked back and forth between the two: the one on the bench remained as still as he had been during their conversation.

Again, she looked at the two Horaces;

(Is it Horaces? Horaci?)

"Dad?"

"The wax sculptor is a bit of a nut." The munching Horace bit down on yet another chip. "He views these things as his literal children, probably because he hasn't got any. He wasn't too fond of the idea of lighting them on fire—or blowing them up."

"Dad?" Terra was still trying to wrap her mind around

everything. She leaned over and poked the wax Horace. "Wait, this is…"

"It's what?" Horace stepped around the bench.

"It's you!" Terra blurted.

Horace crunched another chip. "I don't really see the resemblance."

Terra tilted her head and studied the wax figure. The resemblance was remarkable. It was one-to-one in fact. It would fool his own mother, or daughter as the case may be. Then she remembered the plaque.

The two looked around until she spotted it beneath the bench. They both lay on the floor, and Terra used her phone light so they could read it.

"Horace Blackwater," they both read aloud and in unison. "A prominent agent of horror who discovered greats like Dracula and the tablecloth ghost costume. Died due to not paying taxes."

"Well, *that's* not true." Horace reached for another chip but dropped it.

They crawled their way out from under the bench and sat back up.

"Why are you in this museum anyway?" asked Terra.

Horace brought his free hand to his chin. "You know, the more I think about it, the more I don't think he looks like me," he said flatly.

"That's…"

"On to more important things." Horace offered his bag of chips to Terra. "I was so upset with him that I turned to a vending machine for comfort, but these chips are so bad it's almost scary."

"Uh… okay." Terra grabbed the small, fun-sized bag.

(Even though there's never anything fun about a milligram of chips.)

Before she took one, she noticed the date on the bag. "Um, Dad, these expired seven years ago."

Horace gulped. "Mmm… That would explain a thing or two. Well, the FDA would never allow us to pass off expired food as a scary experience." Horace clasped his hands together. "On to our next adventure then."

"But, Dad." Terra hoped to restart her long-winded monologue.

"Next time, I want you to meet with the perspective client. I'll make an agent of horror out of you yet, if, of course, that's what you want."

Terra nodded. "Yes, of course. You see, I've actually always…"

"Wonderful!"

Terra smiled. Sometimes her dad knew her better than she knew herself.

Horace grimaced. "Now, I think we need to induce vomiting." Horace's face was starting to lose its color.

Terra panicked. "This way, Dad." She guided him to the nearest restroom and…

(Nope, nope! I'm not describing what happened next. Executive decision, the chapter ends right here.)

THE TERRIFYING PLANTMAN

HORACE'S ENTHUSIASM was often compared to a yo-yo by those in the scare business. One minute he would be at rock bottom, but he'd always bounce back with more tenacity than should be humanly possible. Some called it scary, others—well most—called it obnoxious.

In the arc of a yo-yo, Horace was currently at the top of a yo. He didn't look at all like a man who had undergone induced vomiting only a few hours ago. The sun was shining on a bright new dawn in Horace's career, and Terra's, as well. Even though sunshine was frequently seen as bad for those in the horror business, both recognized the bright cheerfulness of the day and ran with it.

The small Romanian town did not have much beyond the wax museum. It was an idyllic small village in a foreign country with beautifully painted homes and narrow roads. Terra was amazed at how green everything was. The rolling hills were always in view, and nature was constantly trying to reclaim where civilization had intruded. Splashes of grass shot out of alleyways, and vines descended from potted plants at every turn.

A tall church stood where several houses intersected, and a small, dark red flower was sticking out of the sidewalk. It appeared to have yellow stuffing inside of it.

Terra knelt inspecting it. "That's an unusual plant."

Horace, a few paces behind her, stopped in his tracks.

"What is it?" Terra asked, having noticed her father's uncanny silence.

A grin swept across his face.

"You had an idea didn't you?"

"Not exactly…but I remembered something. As I recall, there was a gardener who frequently sent me fan mail. Crazed no doubt, but from what I understand, he moved to the Black Sea for the ideal atmosphere for breeding special plants. I never had time to pay him a proper visit…"

"You think we should check this guy out? Do you know anything about him?"

Horace shook his head. "We never met. I believe he mentioned he was an Irishman, or maybe a Scotsman. I'm not sure. He was a big fan of mine, I know that much."

"So, are we going to stroke your ego or find something scary?"

"Terra, dear, whenever we find something scary, my ego will go through the roof."

Terra smirked. "You mean it'll be through the atmosphere."

Along with a small market, a fast-food restaurant, and the wax museum, the small town also had a car rental dealership. It was a modest little shack with a large garage holding a grand total of two cars. The red option and the blue option. The red option was already taken, so they were forced to take the blue.

The dealer insisted on mentioning that it was a small, electric car every time he opened his mouth.

"Oh, the speakers are Bluetooth." Terra realized as she climbed inside.

Horace got in on the passenger side, but the car was so small that he could have easily driven it from that position. "The speakers don't have teeth," said Horace as he tried in vain to get comfortable in what she realized was a clown car, not a Smart car.

"No, Dad, it's a…" Terra stopped and pulled out her phone.

"Going to text and drive now, are we?" Horace folded his arms with a smirk.

"It's easier to show you than to explain."

Horace jumped as a booming song blasted through the car. Terra quickly turned the volume down, but it was still loud spewing words faster than their Smart car could travel.

"What is this anyway?" asked Horace.

"It's K-pop," Terra said with a smile as she pulled out

on the main road—as main of a road as it could be considered. It was littered with potholes and gravel.

"I can barely understand what they're saying," Horace complained.

"You know Korean?"

"N-no—" said Horace.

Terra nearly laughed. "They're singing in Korean."

"Ah, that explains a lot then." Horace slumped in his seat for a moment before shooting back up like a child who just realized he had a question to ask. "Wait, so do you understand what they're saying?"

"Nope," answered Terra.

"Now I'm more confused. They could be singing about a plan to conquer the world, and you wouldn't even know it."

"There's no way." Terra smiled as the song entered an obnoxiously upbeat chorus and turned the volume up to max. "They're just so happy to be singing about that."

Terra clapped along as the vocalists spelled out their plan for world domination, and Horace blurted, "Keep your hands on the wheel. Please."

During a lull in a chorus where a woman was only saying, "oh" "uh-oh" and "oh oh," Terra had a thought. With a grin, she said, "When you thought Bluetooth was actual teeth, I had an idea."

"Oh? What's that?" he practically yelled.

"What about a car that has teeth and eats its passengers? That sounds pretty scary."

"Then just don't get in," said Horace.

"Okay, then what if it was sentient and chased people on its own?"

"Well, that…" Horace stopped.

Terra's smile widened. "Think it might work?"

"Well… Stevie tried something similar a while ago."

She felt as deflated as a three-day-old balloon. "Never mind then…"

As the rocky roads continued, they settled into silence.

Terra occasionally clapped along to the music which made him nervous about her driving. But, in these conditions and the fact that they were going a whopping twenty miles an hour, even if she did strike anything or anyone, they deserved it.

Near the end of the drive, the Black Sea came into view. It was blue just like any other body of water, not black.

(But there's probably a nerd who can tell you why it's called the Black Sea).

"It's beautiful, isn't it?" Terra gazed at the water. A far cry from the crystal-clear oceans found elsewhere, and the beach was not as big or vibrant as Florida, but there was something beautiful about a large body of water, regardless of the quality.

Horace shrugged. "You've seen one ocean you've seen them all."

(Or not, according to some.)

"Before we find this plant man, it's about time we had a talk. About being an agent of horror."

"Yeah?" Terra turned the volume down for the first time since they got in the car.

"There are three things something must be in order to prop it up for the world. First, it must be something which can be scary, or at the very least, appreciated by all ages."

"Like the age on a Lego box?"

"Sure, like Lego," Horace said. "Anyone over ninety-nine doesn't exist or if they do, they're not worth worrying about. Second, it must be able to turn a profit. Finally, and most importantly, it must be a fear which can be overcome."

"Huh?"

"Does that surprise you?"

Terra shrugged. "Not really, I guess it kind of makes sense."

Terra had heard his well-prepared monologue on the role fear plays in each person's life many times, and how he, as an agent of horror, makes fear fun but conquerable, so that people can face their fears in their day-to-day lives with confidence.

The road forced them to a parking lot without a pay meter which was, in and of itself, a win for the two, even if they had no idea where this plant man was. They harassed some locals and tourists alike for information on the plant man. Eventually, a tall, balding man pointed them to a large wooden structure on the sand.

In broken English, the bald man said, "Idiot builds a house every year until it's flooded by high tide."

They thanked him for his help and approached the odd structure. It was not a house, but it was not a commercial building, either. Planks of wood jetted out in awkward directions all along the wall. Neither of them could have guessed it was built to gain the optimal amount of sunlight and be the perfect greenhouse.

(Not immune to flooding though.)

The door was, thankfully, fairly normal looking, but they paused like lawn-care providers knocking on the door of the Mr. greener-grass-than-thou perfectionist.

Horace asked, "Which one of us should knock?"

"You're the agent of horror, why don't you do it?"

Horace sighed. "The things I do for fear." He knocked three times.

Horace worried that knocking would cause the structure to collapse. When no answer came, he knocked again, this time he was much gentler.

"It's open," a Welsh-accented voice echoed from inside.

Horace turned the doorknob, and the entire door fell into the building, leaving the knob in Horace's hand.

"Ah, you're supposed to turn it to the right you beach bums," said the same voice.

"Sorry." Horace dropped the knob so it could join the rest of the door on the floor. "Come on, Terra," and the two stepped over the door and into the laboratory-like greenhouse.

Countless plants and vines littered every possible space. The floor seemed to be some kind of seaweed.

"Look at this." Terra motioned to a red-stemmed green rose. "That's unusual."

Horace spotted a sunflower that was swaying back and forth, as the most bizarre plant he could find.

"Now then, what can I…" the man rounded the corner, appearing right next to a cactus that did not have any needles. He was a stocky man in some sort of janitorial uniform with a harness holding several pots, each filled with dirt, and most contained a sprouting plant.

He shouted, "Mr. Blackwater," and rushed forward. He closed the distance between them faster than should have been possible for a man of his disposition and violently shook Horace's hand.

"I'm so glad you're here, sir. I was worried my letters weren't reaching you."

"Yes, I'm here." Horace hoped the shaking would stop.

The man looked at Terra. "Who's the lass?"

"My daughter."

The man continued to shake Horace's hand but offered his free hand to Terra who shook it twice before pulling her hand away.

"What can I do for you, Mr. Blackwater?" asked the man.

"You can let me go before I puke."

"Oh, yes, of course." He dropped Horace's hand.

"Truth be told," began Horace. "We're here because I'm

interested in getting back into the business, and I always remembered your letters as being… unique. We were in the area, and I thought we'd stop by."

"And you'll be glad you did." He turned to his plants. "Did you hear that boys and girls. Today's the day you'll get your chance."

Horace and Terra exchanged a quick glance as if to confirm that he was, in fact, talking to the plants.

"What exactly sparked your interest in plants, Mr. um…" Terra asked for more information, as well as the man's name.

She's a natural at this. Horace thought with pride.

"Well, ever since I was a wee child, I always had a fondness for the things. They didn't judge me or call me names on the playground. They were my only friends much of my growing up years."

Terra frowned. "How sad."

"But also, it's surprisingly lucrative. You'd be surprised how much people will pay just for soil, let alone the plants."

Horace groaned as a memory he thought was forgotten resurfaced.

Can we just move on from the dirt?

"I notice you have some—unusual plants. How did you create them?" asked Horace.

"Some interbreeding, but mainly genetic modification."

Horace pointed to a plant in the corner. "And you purposely created a tree that produces potatoes?"

"Not exactly." The man put his hands proudly on his belt. The attached plants began to jingle; like bells. "Sometimes, nature is the scariest, so most of the time I just allow it to take over."

"There is wisdom in that…" Horace rubbed his chin. "But I've met a lot of people who have assumed potatoes come from trees, and they certainly wouldn't be scared of flowers having inverted colors either."

"No, I wouldn't expect them to." The man grinned, clasped his hands. "That's why I want you to meet my good friend, Torace, here."

"Why is it called Torace?" asked Horace.

"Eh, just his name, is all."

The man approached a large cactus, and the two followed. It was the one Horace had seen earlier that was missing its pines.

"You can ask him yourself— this is him."

"The cactus?" asked Terra.

"A strapping young lad, ain't he?" The man folded his arms.

"I'm sorry. What's so scary about a cactus? The scariest part would be the spikes, but he hasn't got any," said Horace

"Ah ha, fooled you, didn't he." The man placed a hand on top of Torace's right branch as though it was an arm.

Terra said, "Be careful…" Then she realized that the man was not in any danger.

"You see, unlike normal boring cactuses, or um cactusi,

Torace here grows his pines inside. So, if you give him a good punch or pat his head a little too hard and his skin breaks, you're in for a nasty surprise."

"Okay." Horace was unamused. "So just… don't touch it like you would a normal cactus."

"Ah, but lulled into a false sense of security, some arrogant teen would give him a good punch only to find the ghastly horror that is Torace, the pine-insider-grower!"

There was a long pause.

A *really* long pause.

(*Like the kind of pause when someone calls you by name and asks how you've been, even though you swear you've never seen them before, and you panic trying to recall their name or how you know them, but it just doesn't come.*)

"So, do you have anything else?" asked Horace.

"Does he have something else, he asks?" The man mocked.

"You haven't exactly shown us anything of great worth," Horace whispered so both could hear, but if the man had heard it he refused to acknowledge.

"I'm sure there's some potential here." Terra smiled innocently, albeit her enthusiasm appeared somewhat forced.

"There is not only *some* potential here lass; this *is the* potential."

Horace liked to be the eccentric one, and this man was

giving even him a run for his money. It was starting to get on his nerves. "That doesn't even make any sense."

"To the back room, my friends—if you dare." The plant man rushed ahead of them.

"Come on, Dad. This one's bound to be something good." Terra pulled Horace along.

Horace shook his head. "One day, your optimism will shatter."

Through the back door, one which didn't break when it was opened, was a large dark room.

"Glad you could join us…" the plant man said in the darkness. Suddenly, a light from a match illuminated his face. Reaching out of view, he grabbed something and brought it close. He threw the match inside; it was a lantern that illuminated the whole room.

In the back was a tall shrub-like bush with a vine growing out of it, with two twin roses at the top; a little too perfect for Horace's liking.

"What a beautiful plant," said Terra.

"And the smell can drive insects mad," said the man. "Venessa here is a real charmer, that's for sure."

Terra took a few steps closer but shrieked when the man grabbed her.

"Not a step closer," he screamed. "Or else you'll see why Venessa's such the heartbreaker that she is."

"I take it she's some kind of Venus flytrap?" As much

as Horace hadn't liked anything they'd seen thus far, he couldn't deny his fascination with this one.

"Aye, that's not exactly right. You see, the Venus flytrap is a popular little plant, but there are other carnivorous ones. Most of them attract their prey with a sweet smell and then use a sticky substance to trap them. Venessa's evolved to have a clingier approach."

As he talked, the two couldn't help but notice that Venessa was not simply a shrub but behind it was a large, almost cave like entrance with leaves and pines everywhere. It was like a human stomach only made of plant guts instead of human guts.

"Just how big is she?" asked Horace.

"She's about half the size of this room. But don't let her hear you say that, she's a little vain."

Terra asked, "And what is this clingy approach?".

The man smiled as he moved toward the front of the room. "You see, plants do have a sense of their place in the world. Venessa's got about the same senses as a human, and when something, say a tasty fly or scrumptious little puppy, comes her way and can't resist her beautiful little trap." The man reappeared in the light holding the lantern high with a package of meat in his free hand.

He threw it at the shrub, and it landed just beside it. Almost instantly, a vine appeared from inside the stomach and grabbed it. The vine slowly dragged the package back inside until it disappeared into the leafy stomach.

Horace smiled. "She does offer some promise."

The man chuckled. "Glad you can see the potential. I knew a man like you would. I'd still like to iron out a few things. I'd like to make the smell even sweeter so that humans can't resist it and maybe make the vines a little more flowery."

"We can fictionalize some aspects, but I can already see a Venessa movie. It's not over-the-top scary either which we've seen enough of. I won't lie and say it's a wholly original idea. We've seen plant horrors before."

"But none like this," said the man.

"No," Horace shook his head with a grin. "None like this. And none of them could rise to the level I can take you and Venessa."

"Then it's a success for everyone, right?" Obviously Terra couldn't contain her enthusiasm any longer.

"Oh, I will warn you that she's quite temperamental."

"What?" asked Horace.

As if on cue, perhaps Venessa could understand the language they spoke, a vine reached out as far as it could, startling Terra. It was suspended in the air reaching for the man but came short by just a few inches.

Chuckling, the man said, "Looks like you've become the first person scared by Venessa the Terrible, yet sweet."

Horace sighed. "I'll work on a better name."

Terra instinctually hid behind her father. "But what's it doing?"

"Oh, she's still hungry. Here, I got another pack, girl." He went back to the storage and threw a second pack which was dragged away by a separate vine, while the first vine remained where it was. He retrieved a third pack and threw that inside as well. Then he stretched out his hand and stroked the vine as it seemed to relax somewhat. "You hear that girl? You're going to be famous all around the world."

The vine moved up and caressed the man's face.

Terra looked over to her father who cringed.

"I'll draw up some paperwork and…"

Horace didn't have time to finish his statement, suddenly, the man was jerked forward being dragged by the vine. Horace tried to grab the man's hand, but more and more vines dove out of the monster's mouth. They attacked the man, and one wrapped around Horace's arm.

"Venessa! Honey, let me go! I'll give you another pack!" They seemed to have reached a stalemate in their tug-of-war.

Terra pulled on her father, and they began to win the struggle.

The man blurted, "Wait a moment, what am I doing? Venessa's future is guaranteed, and I could be her first victim. How poetic! How beautiful!"

"I still need you to sign a contract, and no one knows how to control this beast. Please, Mr. um…" Horace stammered, being at a loss for the man's name.

The man laughed. "I never told you my name, did I? Now, I see why… So, you wouldn't get attached to me when I meet my fate. Goodbye, Mr. Blackwater! Goodbye world! Take me Venessa, and you're journey to immortality will begin!" He broke free of Horace's grip.

The vines dragged the terrifying plantman all the way inside. Never to be seen nor heard from again.

Terra dragged Horace as far away as she could. A singular vine still pulled on him, and with the plant man tragically gone, the vines now turned on Horace.

Horace yelled, "Pull harder!" He pushed with all his might to be free, but the vines multiplied, wrapping around each other.

Terra screamed, "The lantern!"

In the chaos, it had been left on the ground. The glass had shattered, but the flame still grew as if demanding a sacrifice even more so than Venessa.

"Terra, wait!" Horace stopped her from going to retrieve it.

"Dad, I know it's important, but your life is more important than this plant. We'll find something else scary. I can't bear to lose you!"

"No, that's not it. I don't want you to leave me." Horace tried reaching the lantern with his foot. "If you let go, Terra, I'll be gone in an instant."

"Oh, I thought you were worried about the plant."

"Of course not! It's a plant."

"But it *is* alive isn't it!?"

Horace's foot reached the tip of the lantern and rolled it back toward them. "Can we save the ethical questions until after we get this thing to stop from killing me?"

Terra grabbed the lantern with her free hand and threw it as far as she could into the belly of the beast.

The lantern exploded inside the stomach causing a chain reaction of flames and shattered glass to shoot out in all directions. The vines that had held Horace were burned at their roots causing the parts by Horace to drop to the ground. He shook them off as quickly as he could.

(But unfortunately, there's something faster than an old man brushing off vines.)

Fire.

The flames were still fighting with Venessa as she shrieked.

(An indication that it could feel pain and thus was alive.)

By now, the fire had engulfed the entire wooden structure that surrounded them.

"Run!" Horace grabbed Terra's hand and made a mad dash for the front door. If it were still standing. he would have kicked it down. but thankfully. it wasn't. The fire burned through all the plants and walls, but the two made it out and ran a few more feet before collapsing onto the sand.

They looked back at the greenhouse as it was swallowed by the flames.

Terra asked, "What about the plant guy?"

"He's…gone the same…way I want to go…That any… horror aficionado would… want to go."

Terra looked at him quizzically. "Huh?"

Horace finally caught his breath "Taken down by his own monster. He'd be happy this way."

"But he…"

"I know. I know…" Horace stood. "This is the danger of our business, Terra." He expected to sound a lot cooler than he did.

"So, I guess we won't be using Venessa as the next big scare?"

"No… It would be insensitive at this point. Even if that is what plant man wanted. Maybe in a couple of years, we'll review this incident with fresh eyes. But for now— we've torched a building with a man whose body is not going to be found by police. I think it's time we leave Romania."

Terra nodded.

And so, the two made a quick exit from the beach and then prepared to leave the country. The fire burned well into the morning, but the next day was high tide, and the ocean swallowed away the wood and ash from the disaster the day before.

***

Somewhere in the sand around where the structure had stood, a sapling began to sprout. No one paid it much mind. After all, it was just a plant, but with each day, it grew ever so slightly taller.

(Okay, so it could be Venessa, but it could just as easily be the potato tree.)

The Disorient Express

Horace and Terra had been through the wringer, so to speak. They were better off than the plant man, but that wasn't saying much.

"The training wheels are coming off. Once we leave Romania and reach England or America, we'll find something so scary it will be the talk of town from California to Transylvania."

Terra smiled, always one to admire her father's unconquerable spirit, especially since she was at the moment in quite a low.

"I'll arrange the travel," knowing she had more experience in that field than her father.

Prior to coming out of retirement, Horace had once planned a family vacation to Key West, which Terra still had scars from.

"A sign that the scary can be memorable, even if it's traumatic," she remembered him saying back then.

On the day in question, Horace accompanied Terra into a taxi. The driver was a stern-looking man with whom

Terra had to communicate through a digital translator. This way, she was able to keep the destination hidden from her father.

"On the one hand, I had hoped we would be able to visit Drac again," Horace said, settling into his seat. "But on the other hand, I'm glad we didn't."

Terra grinned. "He was kind enough to pay for our stay here," she reminded him.

"Drac owes me a lot," Horace said. "I've been good to him, and it's good that he's finally being good back."

"I also have a little surprise for you," Terra said.

"Oh?"

"I know how you hate airplanes, so I booked us on a train."

Horace nodded. "Thank you."

"And not just any train," she added. "The Orient Express."

Horace's eyes bulged. "How did you manage that?"

"Actually, the Count was the one who suggested it."

"When did he mention it?"

"Oh, I've been texting the girls there. We have a group chat now, and I mentioned we would be leaving Romania, and they talked to Dracula who talked to me through them. He's probably about as tech-savvy as you. I booked the tickets online."

"Different generation." Horace folded his arms. "I'd like to see you operate a rotary phone."

"I'd like to see you find a rotary phone," Terra snapped back.

He rested his head against the back of the seat as they rode through the streets of Bucharest

(The capital of Romania and the transport hub to get out of the country).

The Orient Express: the lap of luxury. In his prime, it wouldn't have been much to take a trip like this.

Horace grinned. He was thinking about the idea of spending the next week on a fine train brainstorming wonderful ideas, and he would get to spend all that time with his daughter; a father's dream.

The train depot was packed, as to be expected, but no crowd smelling of sweat from a hundred different nations would stop Horace's optimism. Their two large suitcases were ready to burst from all of their belongings. Horace donned his usual apparel, a dark coat and top hat, and Terra wore multiple layers to save on space in the suitcase. Her light brown coat was about the same length as Horace's trench coat, but not nearly as Gothic.

Terra motioned to the people waiting in line. "Why are they staring at us?"

"Many have just arrived in Romania or are in transit. The one thing the country is known for is vampires, and I happen to look like one."

"Ah," Terra nodded.

When the two reached the front of the ticket line, Terra pulled two tickets from one of a million mini-compartments on her luggage. The man took them, and he immediately squinted. He looked over the tickets then consulted with another man, presumably a manager who existed solely for this one purpose, then sat in a chair hidden from view of customers. Then he could watch cat videos or something else of useless managerial quality.

"Excuse me, ma'am," the clerk said. "These tickets are for the *Disorient* Express, not the Orient Express."

"W…what?"

"It happens all the time," explained the manager. He pointed across the tracks to another booth. "Their ticket stand is over there."

"Next," said the clerk as Horace and Terra were pushed aside by the next customer.

It took them until they were in a clearing well beyond the ticket stand before they realized what had happened.

"The *Disorient* Express." Horace repeated. "That's a Chinese level of knockoff. What's it doing in Romania?"

Terra propped up the handle on her baggage to the highest setting. She sat down and balanced on it as best she could. Tears were starting to form. "I'm sorry, Dad. I really wanted to be helpful and…"

"It's okay, it's okay." Horace put an arm around his daughter. "It's still a luxury train by the looks of it." He cast his eyes at the ticket line. It was shorter than the Orient Express, and no doubt people who had made the same mistake. Both trains looked like the peak of luxury.

They waited through another long line. "Maybe this could be the next big scare," Horace teased.

This time, their tickets were accepted, and they neared the boarding platform when Horace froze in his tracks as though he were in a trance.

"What is it?"

He squinted and looked around the platform but paid no mind to Terra. "There's... a..."

Terra looked in the direction he stared, trying not to assume he was having a stroke. There were numerous people boarding or disembarking the train, but then one person caught her attention.

A tall handsome man, one of the baggage handlers for the Disorient Express. Surely, he wasn't the cause of her father's stroke-like symptoms. Terra looked back at her dad who appeared to have recovered.

"I'm feeling tired. Be a dear and take my luggage to the baggage car, won't you? I'll meet you inside," asked Horace.

All too eager to help, Terra nodded without suspecting any ulterior motive. She took her father's suitcase and started for the baggage man. She didn't think much about him at first other than noticing that he was tall, but as she grew closer, she liked the more she saw.

He had dark matted hair and bright blue eyes like the ocean. The way he lifted each bag with ease and put it on the train was a sign of strong muscles and, of course, a uniform always helped. When he saw her approach, he had a sweet smile that…

(Someone has to write all those cringy details. Just imagine the rest okay? Well, you get the point—he was a hunk.)

"Just two, ma'am?" he asked in a British accent taking the bags from Terra.

Still starstruck by his physique and his smile, she said, "Yes, that's right. Just the two of us."

"Oh? Is it a honeymoon?"

Terra laughed, and the man's smile widened revealing bright white teeth. "Oh no, it's my father and myself. I'm not married." She patted herself on the back for subtly telling him that she wasn't married.

(It really wasn't subtle.)

"Well, welcome abroad the Disorient Express," he said as the two shook hands. "My name's Chadrick. Just holler if you need something."

"Thank you, I will. I'm Terra, by the way." She was eager to make sure he heard her name.

"I won't forget." He grinned and stepped back to gather more luggage.

Terra had to remind herself that the interaction was over and quickly got aboard.

Maybe the Disorient Express won't be so bad after all.

Horace stood in the doorway at the top of the stairs a

few train cars down, blocking anyone from entering. His face wore a dubious grin. He'd seen Terra swoon over boys before, but in this case, it didn't make any sense. It confirmed a suspicion he'd had when he first saw the baggage handler.

Maybe the Disorient Express won't be so bad after all.

The two settled into their adjoining rooms, and the train departed soon after. While he had feigned a sense of tiredness, Horace was, in actuality, chomping at the bit and ready to go. After putting away his luggage and changing into a clean set of his identical wardrobe, he dashed to the dining hall wondering what colorful characters would reside on this knockoff train that rivaled the likes of "KFG" and "Guccy."

It was a small, quaint dining hall that was largely empty. As Horace looked around, he saw only staff except for one man at a table not quite in the center, but not quite in the corner.

The man had a large face or small features, Horace couldn't decide which. His nose did extend out further than most, almost like a mouse or a rat. Horace was going to try to come up with something more friendly—before he started to converse with the man.

Horace approached the table. "Mind if I join you?"

There was no food set out, so the man must have been a recent arrival. He nodded, and Horace took the chair opposite the man.

"My daughter may be joining us, as well, but I saw a

large empty room, and I'd hate to be alone in it." Horace got comfortable in his chair. He leaned back and placed a hand on the table.

"Of course, where are my manners? My name is Horace Blackwater." He reached his hand across the table.

The man smiled, matching Horace's business grin, and they shook hands. "Cheese."

Horace assumed he said "charmed" or something related. It was a train across Europe, after all, so maybe it was an accent or a language barrier that made Horace think he heard "cheese," but he was quite sure that the man did, in fact, say cheese.

"I'm in the horror industry," Horace began the small talk. "I'm an agent of horror. How about you?"

"Cheese."

"Ah, in the cheese business…I see. Are you with a larger company or do you produce the cheese?"

"Cheese," the man repeated.

Horace patted the table and bit his tongue.

The man reached down beside him and pulled up a suitcase. He set it in the middle of the table. He opened it by undoing an eight-digit lock. The grand reveal? Cheese. Every type of cheese under the sun. Cheddar, mozzarella, American, Swiss, and the most pungent: goat cheese. On top of it all was shredded cheese, which appeared itself to be a mixture of multiple types of cheeses.

"Cheese." The man gestured with his hand as if for Horace to partake in his bounty.

"Well, thanks." Horace grinned and took a slice of cheddar cheese.

"Cheeeeeeeese," the man said, nodding approvingly of Horace's decision.

"So, do you just give free samples? Is that your work? What brought you aboard this train?"

"Cheese, cheese, cheese," he spoke the words as if it was a perfectly adequate answer to Horace's question.

"Now wait just a moment here." Horace took a bite of his cheese slice before setting it down on the table. "I'm willing to go along with a joke and all, but how are you supposed to function in regular society if you can only say the word cheese? Do you speak any other languages?"

"Cheese." The man shook his head.

Horace's temper flared. "No really, how did you even get this job?"

"Cheese, cheese." The man reached into his pocket. He produced a wallet, opened it, and revealed a picture of presumably, his family. A wife and three kids.

"Hold on, how did you court this woman? Let alone propose to her?"

The man smiled and pushed his briefcase closer to Horace. "Cheeeese."

"What about when your kids need help with homework or ask you a question?"

The man waited for a moment and inched the briefcase ever so closer.

"Let me guess? Cheese?"

"Cheese."

Horace shrugged and let out a heavy sigh. "Cheese." He picked up the cheddar slice and finished it.

When Horace finished his cheese, the man reached into his suit jacket, pulled out a business card, and slid it across the table.

It had a picture of a slice with the word "cheese" printed in big yellow letters. In small, fine print near the bottom was the word "cheese," over and over again. The phone number was listed as "cheese-cheese-cheese," and the email was "cheese@cheese.cheese."

The man bowed slightly and stood up leaving, Horace with a mountain of questions.

It's not scary in a horror sense, but existentially, it was a little scary.

"Oh, Dad." He was snapped out of his thoughts by Terra's voice. He turned and saw her in one of her finer outfits. She had done up her hair as well.

"Oh, chee…hello." Horace caught himself. Just to be sure though, he repeated, "Hello."

Terra sat next to her father. "Who was that you were talking to just now?"

"It was an interesting man," Horace said. "I don't think he'll be much use to us in our business, but he was nice at least. If I had to guess, his name is Mr. Cheese and…" Horace noticed Terra's eyes were no longer on him but rather something or someone, behind him. He followed her gaze.

Horace suspected it was Chadrick who had captured Terra's attention.

Terra asked, "I'm sorry what was that Dad?"

Horace observed Chadrick exchange simple greetings with the kitchen staff. As if sensing the attention was on him, he made his way over to their table. "Ah, we meet again, Terra." He extended his hand to Horace. "And you must be the father."

"Horace Blackwater." He shook Chadrick's hand.

"Have you two gotten settled onto the train?" asked Chadrick.

Horace said, "Yes, it seems suitable, but I can't help wondering about the deceptive name choice."

The other two stared at each other.

"Oh yes," Chadrick said, momentarily taking his eyes off Terra. "I'm afraid I'm not involved in any of that, though."

"That's a feeble excuse," Horace muttered.

"Where's Mrs. Blackwater, if you don't mind my asking?" Chadrick directed his question to Terra, ignoring Horace as though he were an extra in a low-budget romantic movie.

"Oh, I'm afraid Mother hasn't been around for a long time."

"I'm so sorry to hear," Chadrick said with genuine sympathy.

"Well, it's not like she's dead. There *is* the possibility of parole," Horace added.

"It's okay. I got used to it, and I'm grateful for the relationship I have with my father," said Terra.

"I'm not really in contact with my parents anymore. I just feel too busy."

"That must be difficult," Terra said.

Chadrick shrugged. "I felt lonely for a while, but I get to meet a lot of people working here. The conductor is a bit of a pain, but everyone else is nice."

"Still a lot of people come and go so quickly," said Terra.

"At every station."

"I'm still here you know." Horace felt the metaphorical camera closing in on the two to frame a romantic picture.

Chadrick was still talking to Terra. "There's something special about you. I can't quite put my finger on it, but I actually came here hoping to see you."

Terra shrugged. "I don't know what you mean. I feel fairly ordinary."

"You two literally met twenty minutes ago," said Horace.

"There you are, Chadrick," a deep booming voice echoed from behind them. All three looked over to the source of the voice. It was a fat man in a uniform similar to Chadrick's, but his cap had some frills on it which were most likely supposed to showcase this man's importance but made him look ridiculous.

"Yes, Conductor?"

He spoke directly to Chadrick. "I need you to help Mrs. Dearborn in the Athens-Paris coach, room three."

Chadrick stood. "Baluchi? I think her name was. She said she'd probably call on my services."

"Yes, and she's calling now, so get going. She's the heiress of some pirate or something. She's absolutely loaded, so make sure you treat her kindly." The man looked at the Blackwaters as if he hadn't seen them until now. "Oh, I'm terribly sorry. Is Chadrick keeping you company? Who are you?"

"My name is Horace Blackwater, agent of horror."

The man raised his eyebrows. "Okay, Chadrick you have more important things to do, so get going."

"I'll see you again soon." Chadrick stood, nodded to Horace quickly, and Terra slowly.

Terra slumped in her chair.

Without any further conversation, the conductor ran off.

"Don't worry," Horace said. "I get the feeling Chadrick isn't all he's cracked up to be."

She scowled. "I'm not sure how I'm supposed to feel right now."

"You'll be feeling a lot of that if my suspicions are right," Horace said ominously. He looked out the window for further dramatic effect. They were passing by a mountain, but they went by quickly, and the bright sunlight hit Horace directly.

"Ah, my eyes," he cried.

"You'll be fine." Terra retreated to solitude.

"I could be blind for all you know." Horace held his hands over his eyes. He knew she was walking away.

While his eyes recovered, his mind wandered. The conductor seemed like a mean man. Even though Chadrick was very clearly playing a part, maybe there was some conflict between the two.

Horace grinned.

This could be used to my advantage.

The next few days passed in luxury for most of the passengers, brief albeit romantic encounters for Terra and Chadrick, and much contemplation for Horace.

Horace listened in the dining hall for conversations and most of the passengers, like him, were fooled into thinking it was the Orient Express, but unlike him, most were quite happy with it. Mainly because of a certain man whose name began with "Chad" and ended with "rick." Everyone was completely taken with him.

Horace observed Chadrick too. The whole dining room perked up whenever he entered the room and made his rounds conversing with guests at each table.

Horace was sitting alone when Chadrick approached him. "How are you today Mr. Blackwater?"

"I'm well." Horace lacked the over-the-top enthusiasm everyone else expressed in him.

"Is there anything I can do for you?"

Horace shook his head. "I was thinking of the opposite, actually."

Chadrick's perfect knight's armor seemed to dent if only for a moment. "What do you mean, sir?

"I was thinking of what I could do for you."

"That's very kind of you, Mr. Blackwater, but I'm doing quite well."

Horace cast a glance toward the conductor who was currently yelling at the head chef; something about how adding more water won't hurt the fish. "I'm much more observant than I look." Horace studied Chadrick. "I'm aware that my eyes can't always be trusted."

Chadrick seemed shaken by the remark, but before Horace could elaborate, Terra interrupted them.

"There you are, Chadrick," she said with a smile before acknowledging her father.

Horace leaned back in his chair. "Don't stay out too late you two,"

"It's nothing like that, Dad," said Terra.

Chadrick nodded quickly. "We've found a lot of common interests."

"Sure," said Horace.

The two disappeared and probably began to worry about whether or not Horace was on to their little affair but soon it would be over. Horace knew Chadrick's advances weren't genuine, although, he may not necessarily be to blame for that.

"From now on boil fishes all together. They'll be a school of fish in the pot do you hear? No more wasting time with multiple pots," the conductor yelled.

"Y-yes, sir," the chief said.

Horace had noticed that all of the employees on the train seem to be overworked. Janitors doubled as security, the chiefs doubled as trash collectors, the drivers doubled as engineers, and so on. Except no one seemed to know what Chadrick's official position was. All he did was talk to and help people.

Some of the employees even approached Horace asking him to sign a petition to save Timbo. When asked who Timbo was, they pointed to a fish in the large tank. He was ugly, but Horace had a soft spot for ugly fish. That's a long story for another day. Horace signed the petition, and the employees looked at one another with glee.

"The conductor told us, if we get nine-hundred-nine-ty-nine more, we'll be able to save him," the busboy/toilet fixer said.

"Good luck," Horace said, nodding with a subtle smile.

In the hallway of the luxury car, Horace had planned to turn in for the night, but when he saw an old friend, he stopped. It was Mr. Cheese; Horace hadn't seen him since that first day.

"Cheese..." he whimpered weakly when he noticed Horace spotted him. He looked ill but was standing upright at least.

"Good to see you too," Horace said, moving past the man.

"Cheeeeese," he groaned again.

"I think they have aspirin somewhere. Chadrick would probably know."

"Cheese?"

For once someone who didn't know of Chadrick.

"He's some employee everyone's in love with."

"Cheese cheese?"

"No, I don't dislike him. I just don't like him teasing my daughter the way he is."

"Cheese cheese cheese."

Horace stopped. "Wait, how am I understanding you?"

"Cheese," the man said before turning around.

Chadrick and Terra came through a door from the next train car. They had giddy smiles on their faces, and Horace frowned when he saw they were holding hands.

"CHEEEEEEEEEEESE!" the man yelled upon seeing them. He threw his hand over his heart and fell down.

"Mr. Cheese?" Horace helped him from the ground.

Terra rushed over to help. "Dad, what's happening?"

Horace nodded toward Chadrick. "I think it's your boyfriend's fault."

"Come on, Dad, you can't blame Chadrick for making this guy have a heart attack."

"Cheese cheese," the man whimpered as his pulse became regular.

"I think I can." Horace steadied Mr. Cheese on his feet.

Horace turned to Chadrick. "So, what do you have to say for yourself." But stopped talking once he realized Chadrick was nowhere to be seen.

"Chaddie?" called Terra. "Uh, Chaddrick," she coughed unconvincingly as she corrected herself.

"All the better. Mr. Cheese might have another heart attack if he saw him again, anyway."

"Cheese, cheese?"

"What's this all about?" Terra asked and somehow Horace knew Mr. Cheese had just asked the same question.

"All will be explained my dear, but know that you may not like to hear it."

Terra shivered.

"We need the conductor and, of course, Chadrick himself."

"Cheese?"

"You can be there too."

"Cheeeeese."

"Alright, Mr. Blackwater, what's all this about?" The conductor asked in a way that made him sound like he was important.

(He wasn't.)

The dining car had been emptied of everyone, even the chefs. Hoarce spied one of them smuggle his fish friend Timbo out of the tank.

When Mr. Cheese came in, Horace pointed at Chadrick and explained that "what he saw wasn't real."

The conductor stood in front of the dining area but leaned against the high counter while Chadrick and Terra sat at a table together, appearing on the verge of holding hands. Mr. Cheese sat in front of another table.

Horace stood in his favorite spot, the center of attention.

Mr. Cheese still looked confused.

"I'm sure you're all wondering why I gathered you here," Horace began.

"It's about Chadrick," Terra said, ruining his moment.

Deflated, Horace sighed. "Yes…" He pointed at the conductor. "I think you are abusing a shapeshifter!"

"W-what?" The conductor looked flabbergasted.

Terra narrowed her eyes. "Are you saying Chadrick is a shapeshifter? They aren't real, Dad."

"What are you talking about? Of course they are."

"It's just a make believe thing."

"What about Dracula? He's a vampire, and people think they're make believe."

"Was he actually a vampire? Wasn't that just an act—like his accent?"

"No, he really *is* a vampire." He could see that Terra was struggling with that idea.

"I can prove he's a shapeshifter." Horace directed his comment to the conductor.

"Cheese?"

"That's right," said Horace. "It was you, Mr. Cheese who gave me the final proof I needed. I wonder, Terra, if you would describe what you see when you look at Chadrick."

"Well…" Terra began. "He's a tall man… dark hair…"

"Stop right there!" Horace walked toward the two of them. "He's an attractive young man, isn't he?"

"Y-yes."

"And Mr. Cheese, does this fit in with what you see?"

"Cheese." Mr. Cheese shook his head.

"That's not what I see either," said Horace.

The conductor's eyes widened. "You're all out of your minds."

"Oh really? Then would you describe him? He's right there, so why don't you tell us what he looks like? Be specific." He added those last two dreaded words like a teacher, so he could be sure to dock points for no apparent reason.

"He's… uh…"

"That's enough," Chadrick stood. "It's over, sir." He glared at the conductor. Then his expression softened, and he turned to Terra. "I'm sorry you had to find this out. I really did feel something for you. But since I've gotten to know you, I've been thinking that you deserve to know the truth."

"Wait, what?" Horace asked. "Your feelings for her are fake, aren't they? The conductor was forcing you to appear as something or someone desirable uniquely fit to each person to make them want to come back to this express and increase their profits, right?"

"That's pretty close, Mr. Blackwater,… but it's not the whole truth." Chadrick started his grand confession. "I'm not a shapeshifter, exactly. I'm pretty sure they aren't real. But when I was a child, I upset a witch. Witches are real, but they're not as powerful or usually as evil as your stories make them out to be. I'm sure you had a hand in that, didn't you, Mr. Blackwater?"

"Eh, kinda."

"Well, I had offended the witch of major-but-not-quite-traumatizing-inconveniences. She used up all her power to put a curse on me before she turned into a black and white cat."

Horace had no idea why he mentioned this detail but assumed it would be important for later.

Chadrick continued. "She cursed me to look like something or someone desirable to each person. She convinced me this was a curse, but I didn't believe her for a long time. Then I realized that it affected how people treated me. They didn't know me for who I really was, just for who I appeared to be to them. One day, I met the conductor, and he offered to take me in. I knew he only wanted me for what he saw me as. But I didn't realize to him I was a pile of money and nothing more."

Upon hearing his heart-wrenching confession, the room was silent for a few moments.

"But," he said softly, addressing Terra. "I saw something in you I'd never seen before. It was like the roles were reversed, and I saw something that I desired. I knew it was wrong to deceive you, actually to deceive anyone. So, I won't do it anymore."

"Chadrick…" Terra said.

"Well, good riddance. I don't need you anyway." The conductor stuck his nose in the air and left.

"I have to ask though, Mr. Blackwater. How did you know?" said Chadrick.

Horace smirked. "I had my suspicions since I first saw you, but Mr. Cheese's reaction really sealed the deal. You probably appear as a mountain of cheese to him."

Mr. Cheese pointed and nodded. "Cheese!"

Terra asked, "What did he appear to you as, Dad? Was it something sweet like Mom, or maybe our family all together? Was it a healthy father and daughter relationship?"

Horace was silent for a moment as he weighed his next words very, very carefully. "Maybe it's like the third or fourth most desired thing. I mean, you're a little young for a serious relationship, aren't you?"

"Not really…"

"I'm some kind of monster, aren't I?" asked Chadrick

"Nonsense, you're not a monster. I know that."

"But I look like one to you, don't I?"

"Well yeah. You look like the scariest monster I've ever seen, but that's not really you."

"Cheese!"

"See, even Mr. Cheese agrees," Horace said, even though he knew that wasn't what Mr. Cheese was saying.

"What am I going to do now?" asked Chadrick.

Terra and Horace locked eyes. "I may have an idea."

Horace put his arm around Chadrick's shoulder, not like a future father-in-law but like a business partner. "It must have been *horrifying* to have that curse put on you and realize how it changed your life."

"Not really…"

"It must have been *frightening* to be abused for what others saw you as."

"Kind of."

"There's potential in your story. Probably as a book or something. So, get writing, and as soon as you finish, you call me. Make sure it's a scary book though. Once you're done, we'll send it to some people who will change the entire thing to make it better, and then we'll both be able to make a killing off it."

Horace stopped himself, remembering what the conductor saw Chadrick as.

"You'll be able to live a fulfilling and honest life," he corrected.

Terra added her encouragement. "I know I already told you, but the reason I'm traveling with my dad is to help him find the next big hit in horror culture. It might not be what you want, but maybe it could be a horror and inspirational story."

Chadrick rubbed his chin. "That's not a bad idea."

"Then it's settled," said Horace. "Call me the moment you finish."

Chadrick nodded. "I will."

Everyone turned to a loud commotion from the next

car. They went over to the window and saw a large portion of the staff surrounding the conductor who was tied and gagged. Next to them stood a towering stand holding a fish bowl with Timbo inside.

One of the engineers/drivers placed a large wooden plank on the floor that extended from the side of the train.

"By command of our new conductor Timbo, you have been sentenced to walk the plank!" called the chef.

They all cheered as the conductor was pushed onto the small walkway.

He shook his head violently.

The wooden plank was not as sturdy as one found on a pirate's ship, so, under the combined weight of the con-ductor and his ego, it snapped and he fell to the ground left to the wayside.

The train continued on in a brighter new direction without him.

And as the conductor fell, a glint flashed in the eyes of Timbo.

(It was a dark cynical flash of light for Timbo knew he would rule this train with an iron fist. He knew it was better to be loved and feared equally by his sub-jects, and anyone who dared to challenge his authority would meet the same fate as this bumbling conductor. Human morality would not apply to Timbo the fish. And then he swam a lap around in his fish tank and forgot everything.)

The crew celebrated and began chanting "Timbo" over and over.

"Why don't we become the Timbo Express now?" One of them suggested which was met with unanimous praise.

Horace looked over to Terra and then Chadrick. "I think I'll go congratulate the new captains of the train and make sure we're still on schedule for Paris."

"Cheese, cheese."

"You would like to join me, Mr. Cheese?" asked Horace. "I wonder if the fish likes cheese?"

Horace and Mr. Cheese excused themselves leaving Terra and Chadrick alone.

"Thank you," said Chadrick. "For helping me come to my senses."

"Yeah… I'm sorry I have to go now."

"No, you should go. Your father will need your help. But I won't forget you. I'll have to change your name, but I plan on writing about you in my memoir for being the reason I was able to come out of the darkness and accept my curse."

"You did all that yourself though," Terra said as the two gravitated toward each other like celestial objects in space.

They could both feel the urge to draw even closer with their lips, but the door opened suddenly, and they flew *apart* like celestial objects in space.

Horace walked in. "They'll take us to Paris still, but fish is officially off the menu for the rest of the trip,"

"O-*fish*-aly?" Chadrick said with a grin.

Terra sighed. "Maybe we should see other people."

MUNDANE SCARE

At the Paris airport, Horace and Terra waited for their delayed plane.

"Are you over your brief romantic escapade?" asked Horace

There were too many people in the terminal for it to be half empty, but it looked too sparse to be half full.

Terra glared at her dad. "I don't want to talk about it."

"Well, when you're older, you'll understand and be ready for the real thing." Horace reached into his suitcase. He pulled out an eye mask and placed it over his head.

It was black, of course, so now he was absorbing a small vacuum of light around him with his black coat, hat, and blinders.

"Dad, I'm in my twenties. I think I'm ready for the *real* thing. The problem is finding the right person."

"We can discuss this later. I'm trying to sleep." Horace slid a little in his chair, so his head was lower than it should be.

"How did you and Mom meet?"

"Sleep," Horace said once again, refusing to answer.

After a few minutes had passed, Horace said, "You know a good number of people meet their significant other at work."

"Is there a *significant* reason you bring this up?"

"Of course!" Horace stood, sleep mask still on. "It's so simple, it's genius. Why hasn't anyone thought of it sooner?"

"You okay, Dad?"

"Yes, where are we flying to? New York?"

Terra nodded, but Horace obviously couldn't see her.

"I need to make a call." Horace dashed off to the nearest phone station, forgetting he had a cell. He nearly tripped over multiple children, and it wasn't until he was on the phone that he removed the eye mask.

Horace loved his secrets and refused to tell Terra what his "grand idea" was for the entire flight. It was a horrible flight, too, especially with two major factors: one, Horace hated airplanes. When he fled the United States for tax evasion, he traveled by boat and then train.

The second factor which added a sense of anxiety to their flight was they didn't know if Horace would even be allowed to land in the country.

If Horace and Terra were smarter, they would have done more research, but several years had passed since Horace's legal trouble. In all of his time in Romania, he had never been contacted, and the IRS did repossess his entire house and anything he left there. Surely, his debts were paid, but he couldn't be certain.

Immigration did ask he and Terra a lot of questions upon landing, but they passed through with only a thorough baggage and body inspection.

"Enjoy your time in the States," the officer had told them. He seemed to have a minimal amount of disappointment in his voice when they didn't find any contraband on them.

"What were they looking for anyway?" Terra asked once the two were on their way with luggage in hand.

"Drugs, illegal money, weapons, and more than an ounce of liquid."

"Scary stuff," Terra commented.

"Not scary enough," Horace said, thinking back to his idea. They were able to hail a taxi, and Horace gave the man an address which he immediately entered into his phone.

"What's so special about that place?" asked Terra.

"You'll see."

Terra was expecting something grand or even something unique, but when the taxi driver stopped, they were in front of an ordinary office building. It was a little run-down but not to the point where it looked haunted.

The two gathered their luggage and walked to the front door.

"Is this where we're staying?"

"We have a lot of work to do here, so yes. We'll have to get some beds brought in, but let's see what they've left us."

A large banner next to the door said For Sale. Horace put his hand behind the banner and pulled out a small key. Then he removed the banner.

"You didn't buy this place, did you?"

"I got a discount," he said with pride. "There are people who are indebted to me, you know."

The key took some finagling, but he got the door to open.

They stepped inside.

"So, you bought an office building…" Terra was unable to see where this was going. "How much renovating does this need?"

"It shouldn't need much," Horace said as the two moved into the lobby. A large wooden desk stood against the far large wall; the finish was peeling in multiple loca-tions. A faded red chair was behind one side of the desk, but the other side was left empty.

"Time to see if the elevator works," Horace said as the two entered.

"Can we stay on one of the higher floors? The view might be nice."

"Certainly." He hit the button for the top floor and noticed it was a little sticky. It wasn't anything a wet cloth and some elbow grease wouldn't take care of.

Light jazz music started as the elevator slowly ascended.

"We'll have to change that." Horace sighed. "But then again,… it is rather mundane, I suppose."

"Mundane?"

Horace clapped his hands together. "Yes. Tell me, Terra, why did you want to join me, again?"

At first, she thought he had forgotten or was about to start a serious conversation, but then she remembered the over-the-top nature of her father and knew this was part of his grand reveal. "I wanted to spend time with you."

"But what were you hoping to run away from?"

"Run away from?" It wasn't how Terra would put it, but she knew he was trying to lead her answer down a certain path. "I guess I was running away from not having a good family relationship. I mean, after what happened with Mom and not seeing you for a few years, I was…"

"I didn't ask for the sappy version. You were running away from a mundane life, weren't you?"

"Not really…"

"But you were. You didn't want to start an ordinary life using your English degree for… um—whatever it's used for, and you wanted a life of excitement. Just like me when I first became an agent of horror."

It still wasn't accurate to how Terra would put it but she was starting to understand her father's idea with this place.

The elevator doors opened, although, jazz music continued to play. Horace rushed out like a child who had been confined on a three-hour car trip. "Ah, beautiful," he said as he saw the generic-looking office building layout. "They left the cubicles for us."

"Yippie…" Terra said sarcastically, stepping out of the elevator.

She gravitated to the nearest window, fully expecting a picturesque view of the entire city but found she was looking directly into the neighboring office building. She frowned. To make matter worse, the windows in the two buildings were off-centered.

"Why the sad look, dear?"

"Nothing, just a little disappointed, I guess."

"Well, find a place to rest for the night, and tomorrow we work on making the mundane scary."

"That's your plan?"

Horace nodded. "It's something so perfect and so simple. I'm surprised that no one thought of it before. We'll make staplers into werewolves, and each cubicle will be a dungeon. This may even outdo the tablecloth ghost costume in terms of popularity!"

"Okay, Dad," Terra said, beginning to smile.

Maybe this idea really will work…

"Well, I call this cubicle." Horace placed his hand on the side wall.

"Do you think we could get sleeping bags or something at least?"

Horace rubbed his chin. "Why not? Let's splurge. You can stay here. Enjoy the view." Horace gestured to the useless window.

"It's not really a view."

"On the contrary, it's such an ordinary view. Let it inspire you further to my idea."

Terra smiled. "Uh-huh."

Several weeks passed as the two worked hard from sunrise to sundown and then some. Much of Terra's work was restoring the office to its former—well, not glory, but former status as a regular office building. She sometimes glanced across the window and watched the people in the normal office building for reference, but sometimes they stared back and it became awkward.

Terra had helped in all the preparations, but in her eyes, all they had done was make it look like it did originally. She knew the point was that the ordinary would be scary, but there was no twist to it. Nonetheless, Horace insisted they were ready and scheduled an opening night. They took out ads of all kinds and hung an elaborate banner on the side of the building.

On the big night, Horace rolled out a red carpet in front of the door, and the lobby was turned into an intricate maze with those line dividers, with the ropes and stands using as much space as possible.

Terra didn't know what they were called but had never bothered to look it up.

Terra pointed to all the theatrics. "Doesn't that go against the whole idea of what we're doing?"

She and Horace had even dressed up; well, Horace's attire looked a little cleaner than usual.

He waved a hand dismissingly. "We're presenting the ordinary in a brand-new light. Besides, the lobby isn't part of the experience."

The two went to the front doors together to open them to the public.

"You've come so far, Terra," Horace said with a tear beginning to form. "Are you ready for your grand debut as an agent of horror?"

She nodded, and with both their hands on the door handle, they pushed it open.

"Welcome to the Mundane Scare!" called Horace.

The crowd was not what they had expected primarily because it was not a crowd. There were four people, but one of them was a homeless man sleeping on the bench just outside the door so neither Horace nor Terra were sure if they should count him.

At the front of the line was a young couple probably around Terra's age with hesitant smiles, and behind them was an older man in a dark brown coat and fedora.

"Come right this way," Horace said with no noticeable loss of enthusiasm.

Terra led the first three through the maze for several minutes until they decided just to duck under all the tape and make their way to the front.

"And would you like to join us?" Horace said to the homeless man.

He looked at Horace for a few moments in silence before answering, "You talking to me?"

"Yes, of course. We have a night full of terror ahead!"

The man waited again before answering, "Nah… I'm good."

"So be it."

"You know my life is pretty scary as is. Mind if I tell you about it?"

Horace closed the doors on the man. "Not at all." There's always someone who tries to tell him their life story whenever he has these elaborate outings.

Horace navigated the maze for a few minutes longer, but this time had advice from the others trying to guide him. Ultimately, he gave up and went under the ropes.

Horace moved behind the front desk and pulled out a massive stack of paper. "Now if you'd all be so kind as to sign the waiver, we can get underway."

Terra asked, "How many did you print?"

"This is just one." Horace pushed it across to the young man. "Here you go." He pulled out another large stack giving one to the woman and then doing the same for the older man.

"We're not signing away our firstborn or anything, are we?" the young man asked.

Horace chuckled. "No, nothing like that. Your second born, maybe."

"Come on, let's just hurry it up." The young woman skipped to the end and signed.

Reluctantly, the young man did the same.

Horace held out his open hand. "And the fifty-dollar entry fee?"

"Fifty dollars?" the man shook his head. "I thought this was going to be a cheap date." He pulled out his wallet and surprisingly had a fifty-dollar bill which he placed on the counter.

"Per *person*," Horace emphasized.

The man sighed and then produced another fifty-dollar bill.

"And is your paperwork done?" Terra asked the older man.

"No, there are a few clauses I'm concerned about. I'd like to give this a little more reading first."

"No problem. Now then, let's begin our journey," Horace said as he, Terra, and the couple got onto the elevator.

No words were spoken on the ride up.

When the doors opened, Horace was the first to step out and began guiding them through the room. The stereotypical office workspace had been fully restored with multiple cubicles, a large glass-walled conference room, and of course, a water cooler, which was the oasis in a sea of misery. However, if anyone tried to drink from it, they would discover it was salt water. Bright floodlights illuminated the room causing everyone to wince.

Horace pointed to the nearest cubicle. "Now then, I need you to present a twenty-minute presentation on our sales reports for the last five years to the board of directors. You have fifteen minutes, and that computer to help you."

Without a moment's delay, the young man jumped into his office chair and began to work. The computer booted up slowly, and when it finally came on, it asked him to update to the latest version and also aggressively informed him that the virus protection on the computer had expired.

Horace walked the young lady to the next cubicle. "You signed that you were okay with workplace sexual harassment, so this speaker will occasionally spit out disparaging remarks. You will need to staple together all the reports that have been brought in, however, do not mix them. They are not sorted in any way for you and can vary in page count from one to thirty-nine. The header on each page will tell you which report it belongs to, but the printer was running out of ink while these were printed. You have twelve minutes."

Panic filled her eyes when she picked up the stapler. It looked like it was from the fifties. She had to use her entire body weight to get the staple to eject. The stack of papers truly was unorganized. If she threw them all over the floor, she would probably have better luck going through them.

Terra was nervous about a potential lawsuit over the sexual harassment coming through a small speaker, but Horace was pure in heart (once you went deep enough into his heart) and being a man meant he hadn't faced the kind of abuse he had planned on using for this makeshift non-haunted house. He had looked up a list of quotes that he assumed were sexual harassment but were actually insults made by toddlers.

The speaker had said things like: "You throw like a girl." and "You smell like bad feet." The worst one, however, managed to get a tear to roll down the young woman's cheek: "You aren't even invited to my half-birthday party."

Horace pulled Terra aside. "You check on the young woman, and I'll check on the young man."

Terra nodded, and the two went to their assigned roles.

Only ten minutes had passed when Horace approached the young man. Part of the scare was that there was no timer set, so the man was not going to receive the full fifteen minutes. "How's it going?" Horace asked.

The man shook his head. "This isn't what I expected," the man confessed. "I brought my girlfriend since I thought this was going to be a haunted house, and she'd get all scared, and I could protect her while she stays really close to me and all that."

Horace rolled his eyes. "I meant the progress on the project?"

"It's…coming along. This is more of an existential fear than a spooky fear, though."

"It's not Halloween, so I wouldn't think you would expect a spooky fear. You have a minute to finish your project. And I'll disable solitaire on your computer for the final minute."

"NO!"

Terra's conversation with the young woman had gone slightly better. "How are you doing?" She asked as the woman raced between two piles of papers.

"I'm stressed! I don't think I can do it in time."

"It's okay take, a deep breath," Terra said. "The fear you're feeling will help you empathize with your boyfriend after this event. See fear is a good thing."

"I know, but I was kind of hoping we'd be together throughout this. I wanted him to think I was scared and try to act all big to try to protect me. I thought this was going to be a romantic date, not something to remind me about work." The woman was on the verge of tears.

The supposed abuse line chimed in through the speaker, "Your mother is so fat scientists stopped calling Pluto a planet because of her."

"You have another minute," said Terra. But it only seemed to cause the woman more stress.

Horace and Terra reconvened and shared how their experiences had gone. "Dad, I don't see how this is working," said Terra flatly.

Horace explained, "I've always known that the unnatural spooky fear most of our products and clients give is to distract people from real-world fears, but somehow, I thought this would be an exception whereby tapping into real-world fear and making things so absurd in the process, people wouldn't help but laugh at their own fears by comparison."

Surprised, Terra said, "Wow, you actually had a thought process for this idea."

"And what is that supposed to mean?" Horace suddenly realized the minute was up and clapped his hands together to announce time to stop.

"I need those reports, and you all need to prepare to present your presentation."

The young man stood abruptly and glared at Horace. "No, this is ridiculous. Come on, we're leaving." He grabbed his girlfriend by the arm; she threw her stacks of reports on the ground.

(She probably meant it as an act of defiance, but since she had stapled most of them together, her work wasn't undone.)

"This isn't fun, it's crazy," she said.

"Of course, it is," Horace said. "It puts into perspective our…"

"Yeah, that's too many words for me. Let's go." The young man took his girlfriend's hand, and the two hurried down the stairs.

Horace and Terra got into the elevator. "Let's go check on the other one," he said.

This time they did talk on the way down. "They'll be more willing to stand up to their unreasonable bosses at work now," Horace theorized. "We have helped them, and eventually, they'll realize this and become grateful for their time here. Or their shared trauma will bring them closer together."

Terra sighed. "Or they could leave a bad review and kill any traction this place could have had."

"You're supposed to be the optimist," Horace said as the doors opened. The man from before was gone too. "Coward," muttered Horace

No one else came, so they decided to assess the damages in the morning and turn in for the night.

"We have… three reviews?" Terra said, looking at her phone. The first was a one-star review with a lengthy essay about how horrible of a time their experience had been. The second was a two-star review that said at least the workers were nice, and the third review was also two stars but simply said "grate place. Lots of fun."

Terra smiled. "Not every idea can be a winner."

Horace groaned. "On the bright side, if those two ever have kids, we legally own their second born."

The Identity Theft of Dr. Frankenstein

THE OFFICE BUILDING SCARE was too ahead of its time, or so Horace decided. So, they sold it for quite the bundle, and it was converted into an apartment building that would charge exorbitant prices for a room with a barely functional bathroom.

Even with their expenses surprisingly high despite the failure, they didn't even entertain the idea of staying in New York. Not with those prices. So, they drove for most of the day until they reached a small bed and breakfast in Vermont.

The place didn't look like it had changed much since the days of George Washington. The lush landscapes and beautiful pinewood smell made for an idyllic picturesque place. Of course, Horace stood out a lot in such a location, but it didn't bother him.

Waiting was not Horace's first choice, but after running across the world and doing a few different ideas he was, for the first time, fresh out. Sure, he still had some vague ideas in the back of his head, but they were not bursting out of his brain like bolts of lightning or forcing their way out of the clouds. They were still building and brewing until either a new idea would appear out of nowhere or one of those ideas would culminate and strike when it was ready.

He sat peacefully on the patio in a rocking chair while the breeze blew across his face. Dark storm clouds gathered in the distance, but the wind was not too strong and the temperature was just right. Such a melancholy atmosphere demanded a little retrospection. He thought about everything he and Terra had gone through since starting their journey.

There is still potential in wax.

But his passion had been turned away, and he needed a new twist in order to reignite it. He didn't want to think about plants for a long time, let alone boxes of dirt. Chadrick had sent a letter detailing how he had finished the first paragraph of his book, and Horace resigned himself to the fact that Terra would have to continue that endeavor well after he had kicked the bucket. As for Horace's own ideas, he began to realize just how preposterous his most recent attempt had been. If he were to do it again, he would have added more role play: like an angry-looking man shouting at the people the whole time about deadlines and quotas. There was, after all, always next time.

"Excuse me? Mr. Blackwater?" A man's voice echoed through the air.

Horace looked around to identify the source. A tall man, who looked like he belonged on a food brand label, stood next to Horace's chair.

His approach was so quiet that Horace was startled by how close the man had gotten without his noticing.

Horace looked up. "Yes?"

The man was silent for an unusually long period of time. He seemed to be waiting until enough tension formed and for Horace to say something again. But just as he did, the man interrupted.

"There is a telephone call for you."

"You guys still have a landline?" Horace said, getting to his feet.

"We say it's a landline for billing purposes, but it is just the boss's cellphone."

"How does that even save money—never mind. Who is it?"

"He said he was an acquaintance of yours."

"That's *really* specific." Horace followed the man to the lobby. He braced himself for the worst. It was likely a rabid fan or eccentric person with "a great idea" which Horace had heard a million of and barely 10 percent of them were good.

It might even be a repeat of that plant fanatic.

Horace took the phone. "Horace Blackwater here. Do you know me or did you lie to the receptionist?"

The voice was frail but quick to answer back, "Well, we haven't actually met."

Horace's hand went for the End Call button, but as his finger lingered over it, the man said something that made him pause.

"But we know a lot of the same people. My name is Dr. Victor Frankenstein."

"Frankenstein?"

Frankenstein and Dracula entered the horror scene at around the same time, but Horace was Dracula's agent, so someone else was Frankenstein's. Horace knew all about him, and it was a good horror story. He had a fondness for Dracula, but he didn't have anything against Frankenstein. Except, of course, that he wasn't his agent.

"I understand you're back in the business. I saw your ad for the mundane scares. Was that it?"

"Yes, we had to shut our doors prematurely. I can put you on our email list if you're interested in our eventual comeback."

"No, no. I just wanted to talk to you."

"Who's your horror agent? You know there's a noncompete clause, right?"

"Well, that's part of my issue. I believe my contract has expired with them, and anyway, and they won't return my calls."

Horace rubbed his chin. He was sorry to hear about it, but he also knew it could mean something big for him.

"I could use some help. It's a complicated issue, and I know you might not be able to do anything, but will you at least hear me out? I'm on a pay phone right now, so do you mind if we meet in person? They charge me for every syllable."

"Sure."

How did he find a pay phone?

Horace gave him their address, and Dr. Frankenstein said it would take him a few hours by bike to get there.

As soon as the call was over, Horace rushed to find Terra who had been playing croquet on the front lawn with one of the other clientele in the hotel.

"Look, Dad. I'm winning," she shouted as she held a mallet in each hand and spun her arms like a cartwheel knocking two balls with one swing. Each went on to go nowhere near metal hoops. Horace assumed they were the point of the game.

The old woman competing with her cursed under her breath. "I'm already at fourteen points, and she didn't get any from that. I hate games that make the person with the lowest score win." In frustration, she threw her tennis racket on the ground.

It was only then that Horace noticed a curling broom, a hockey puck, and several darts strewn about the lawn. "What game uses all this?"

"I won!" Terra said, laying her mallets on the ground.

"Right. Congratulations on winning whatever game this was. We have a visitor coming."

Horace explained the whole phone call.

"Frankenstein? *The* Frankenstein?"

"I can't imagine why his horror agent would drop him,

but if we can secure a deal with him, it'll be like a gold mine. We won't even have to work for our success. With a name like Frankenstein, people will come from all over no matter what we do."

"We could even do a horror reality TV show." Terra suggested.

"Yes, we could even do—well, let's see what his problem is first and then sort out the details."

Horace and Terra waited in the mini parking lot of the hotel watching in both directions for cyclists. As soon as they saw one, they went out onto the road to greet them, but the angry rider yelled at them nearly running over Terra in the process.

"Gluts don't look this good by stopping to talk with any wack I see!" they heard him yell as he rode away.

Feeling defeated, they returned to their spot and waited for someone who fit the image they had in their mind for Frankenstein. Such a person never came.

The closest they got was a sickly man who peddled at an astonishing two miles an hour but managed to keep his balance. The only reason he was the closest to the description was because, as it turned out, he was Dr. Frankenstein.

"Mr. Blackwater?" The man practically fell off his bike.

Terra helped him dismount and then stood close by as it looked like he might tip over just like his bike did which neither one of them grabbed when he was off.

He extended his hand. "Dr. Victor Frankenstein. Nice to meet you."

"You're Frankenstein?" Terra said in disbelief.

Horace shook the man's hand. "I'll admit, you're not what I was expecting."

"I thought he'd be taller."

"I thought he'd look more like a monster."

"No, no!" The man burst with anger. "That's my problem. *I'm* Frankenstein! I'm not a monster, but my creature claims *he* is Frankenstein!"

Horace tied Dr. Frankenstein's bike to the front door with a zip tie so that it wouldn't be stolen, and the three headed inside to the nice, air-conditioned lobby.

"Get him some water," Horace suggested, but not doing it himself.

Terra went off to fulfill her father's request as the doctor let out a heavy sigh and sank deep into the vortex that was the lobby chair. Once Terra returned, Frankenstein eagerly gulped down the glass.

Horace asked, "So, let me get this straight…your problem is that this monster is using your name?"

Dr. Frankenstein nodded. "Not just my name. He's using my bank accounts, my old high school ID, even my Twitter!"

(Well actually it's X now.)

"He's stolen my identity, and he's used it for all sorts of outlandish things. I keep getting emails about a rewards program he's enrolled in for an ice cream shop in Ontario.

I've also lost everything. My home, my car. They're all his now, or so he claims. Worst of all, he's using my money to pay for a premium service on some dating app called '*Mushy Monsters.*'"

Horace almost spit.

Terra grimaced. "That's despicable."

Horace could feel his chest tighten. "What masochistic soul would willingly subject themselves to the premium service on *Mushy Monsters?*"

"You know about that app?" Dr. Frankenstein asked.

"We're not talking about that," Horace said with such gusto he stood up drawing the attention of everyone in the lobby.

"Um, Dr. Frankenstein?" Terra said. "Haven't you gone to your lawyer about this?"

"I have, but you know what he said? He said I didn't look anything like Frankenstein!"

"I take it you never met him before?" Horace said calmly, sitting back down.

"I did meet him once, but everyone is so confident that the monster I created is Frankenstein, and if there's one thing people hate more than identity theft, it is being proved wrong! All it would take is a simple search online to figure out that the monster never had a name."

"Maybe he just wants a name," Terra, ever the sympathetic, said.

And like all sympathetics, she was ignored.

"How did this happen anyway?" asked Horace.

"Well, I only have one password for everything, so that's probably how."

"I mean you can't be expected to have memorized fifty-something passwords," Horace interjected.

"I know, right?"

"Why not use a notebook to write down all your passwords?" Terra suggested.

"Please, I am a scientist," Dr. Frankenstein said with what small amount of pride he had left. "I must strive for peak efficiency in everything I do. Writing things down takes time. Memorizing things takes up brain cells. I have the resources for neither."

"So, with all fairness," Horace said. "What do you want us to do?"

"Dad," Terra said gently, hitting her father.

(it wasn't gentle according to Horace.)

"This has nothing to do with us. And I'm not a lawyer. I'd go kicking and screaming into law school."

"I know. I just thought you might have experience with something like this." Dr. Frankenstein sighed. "I have nowhere else to go."

"Have you contacted your parents?" asked Terra.

"They think the monster is their son, now."

Terra felt a tear well up in her eye. "Come on, Dad. We've got to help him."

"Oh, you know we will." Horace grinned. "After all, there's very good sequel potential here. Just think about the modern commentary this event could give on identity theft in an increasingly more digital age. What it means to be human is always a serious and sometimes scary question, but in a digital age, you could disappear with a simple FBI agent falling asleep with a finger on his backspace key."

"I don't think that's how that works," said Dr. Frankenstein.

Terra folded her arms. "*And* we're going to help him because it's the right thing to do."

"And because it's the right thing to do." Horace repeated. "So, where's this monster now?"

"He's currently trying to take out a loan with some bank in New York. He always talked about building a mansion and settling down in South America when he was strapped to my gurney."

"When he was what?" Terra looked surprised.

"When I was creating him and planning to parade him around to the scientific community! Then I met a horror agent who was much more interested in my achievement from a Halloween perspective."

"Well, that's how I'd look at things," said Horace.

"The rest is history until he stole my identity. That is the present."

"What did he think about it? Did he want to be viewed as a monster and scare people?" asked Terra.

"No, I think he just wanted me to make him a girl-friend and then start a family," said Dr. Frankenstein.

"Terra, why do you keep taking the monster's side? Did you forget that he stole the good doctor's identity?"

"Well, no, but I mean he doesn't have a name, and he didn't want to be a monster. Maybe he felt like he had no choice," said Terra.

"Of course, he had no choice. I made him. He's my creation and therefore my property."

Horace and Terra shared an uncomfortable glance as they realized he might not be a good doctor after all.

Horace was upset about the long drive ahead of them especially since they had just come from the New York area. Matters were not helped when Terra and Dr. Frankenstein spent the entire ride trying to find things they had in common. They eventually found one, and Horace had wished that they hadn't. They both liked an obscure North Korean band and then demanded that their music be played on max volume while the two attempted to sing along in a language neither one of them understood.

"You'll love it, Dad," Terra said gleefully as she began to play it from her phone.

Horace knew he wouldn't love it.

Unfortunately, by this point, they were too far along and had entered the gridlock of the Tristate area, and Horace could no longer speed up the car and send it off a cliff or into oncoming traffic to end his pain.

He endured and he endured bravely.

Once they found parking…

(you don't want to know what happened)

…they had to create a plan, and since they wasted all

their time singing to sounds that Horace refused to call music, they didn't have any ideas.

Dr. Frankenstein climbed out of the car. "I haven't been able to confront him, so maybe a direct assault will solve our problem?"

"You didn't even try to talk to him before?" asked Horace.

Dr. Frankenstein shook his head. "I have no means of travel. I have no email or phone since he owns everything. My only hope is to find him in person, but he's always been too far away for me to pedal to him."

Terra scowled. "So, we'll just stumble across him in New York? One of the most populated cities in the world."

"I do have some ideas," said Dr. Frankenstein. "He would often mumble during experiments about how he wanted to skate on ice. He watched the Olympics one year, and I guess that was his favorite event, so he might be at one of the famous ice rinks in the city."

Terra paused for a minute. "That does narrow it down, but they might have closed for the night already."

"But that may not necessarily stop a monster like him from getting on the ice," protested Horace.

"That's right!" Dr. Frankenstein's mood seemed to lighten.

Terra let out a sigh, and the three went to the most famous ice rink, according to Horace, in all of New York, at the Rockefeller Center. A large crowd was waiting at the entrance as a commotion seemed to build. The three made their way to the front to see the rink empty except for a very tall figure bundled from head to toe in winter gear.

"That's him," Dr. Frankenstein yelled. He jumped past security and fell onto the ice. Having already failed to stop one intruder, the security did nothing to stop Horace and Terra.

"Are you sure that's him?" Terra called as they stumbled across the ice.

Dr. Frankenstein yelled, "It has to be!"

The tall figure turned its head toward them; he was incredibly ugly. The kind of face only a mother could love, and unfortunately, because he was created by Dr. Frankenstein, he didn't even have a mother to love it.

"Doctor?" He spoke in a booming voice.

"Finally." Frankenstein tried to bring himself to a stop on the ice, but he drifted to the left. "We found you."

There was a chill in the air as Horace, Terra and, to some extent, the crowd even seemed to realize the significance of this encounter. On one side of the ice was Horace, Terra, and Dr. Frankenstein. On the other side, all alone, was the monster who claimed his name was also Victor Frankenstein. Unfortunately, there was one person who didn't recognize the significance of the events, nor was he even aware that there were people still on the ice.

Of course, this wouldn't matter if it was just one person, but considering this *one person* happened to be the Zamboni operator, a highly esteemed and sought-after qualification, it did matter. It was time for the regularly scheduled cleaning of the rink, and despite multiple warnings that there are people on the ice, the proud Zamboni operator continued because he had headphones on playing heavy North Korean pop music.

He drove straight onto the ice causing, a fissure between the two groups. It was a metaphorical fissure, but like a real one, they could no longer cross the middle out of fear of being swallowed alive by the merciless Zamboni machine.

"What you want doctor?" the monster bellowed over the noise of the Zamboni machine.

"I want my life back!" yelled Frankenstein.

"It's my life now! I never asked to be created! You made me, and you have to suffer consequences doctor."

"No one ever asks to be given life," Terra yelled.

(She was trying to find some sense of reasoning. But it was far too complicated and philosophical for this story so to keep it short she added.)

"But everyone gets it, and you have to treasure what you have, not what other people have."

"Can we just agree to talk over dinner?" Horace offered.

"Only if doctor pays for it," the monster answered back.

"You *stole* all my credit card information. I can't pay for it," yelled the doctor.

"Don't you carry cash, doctor?" the monster hollered as the Zamboni passed directly in front of them. It moved in a line back and forth, slowly going across the ice causing the monster to step back and the group to step forward.

"Of course, I don't carry cash. I live in the twenty-first century!"

"Too bad for you, doc," the monster yelled. "No deal!"

Horace sighed. "*I'll* pay for it."

"No. That was not part of deal."

The doctor shouted, "Listen here, you nitwit!"

Horace skated over to Terra. "Keep them talking. I have an idea." Then he skated off the ice. The security harassed him, but then they let him go without any repercussions.

"Don't agitate him," Terra said, moving closer to Dr. Frankenstein as the Zamboni allowed them to move up again. "We want to reach a solution that helps everyone here. Name-calling and playing the blame game is just going to make him more entrenched in his worldview."

"Nonsense girl," the doctor said. "This is how things are done in the scientific community. The smartest person, me, is always correct!"

"If you're so smart, how come you gave all your accounts the same password?" The monster taunted.

"Because I don't have…"

"That was a rhetorical question. You're stupid."

"I literally made you from simple materials and body parts I found in a grocery store and a cemetery. I am the greatest genius the world has ever known."

"Dumb-dumb say what?"

"What does that…"

"Dumb-dumb said it!"

"Listen here, you doorknob!"

"Idjit!"

"Pillock!"

"Poo-poo head!"

"Nincompoop!"

"Your IQ is negative infinity."

"Yours is negative infinity minus one."

"Yours is minus two."

It was not Terra's plan but the bickering continued to go on for several minutes. All the while she kept wondering why neither one suggested negative infinity minus negative infinity, but then she realized that subtracting a negative number from the same negative number would always equal zero. After going to thirty, however, they began another onslaught of mean name-calling.

Then the monster was backed up against the wall as the Zamboni driver continued to clean that side of the rink.

And then it happened.

An ominous ringtone sounded from the monster's pocket. It was his turn to call the doctor something juvenile, but he had lost all interest when he heard the buzzer.

His eyes nearly bounced out of his head, which given his origins might be possible. "HOT WITCH IN MY AREA AND SHE MATCHED WITH ME!" he yelled so loud that even the Zamboni driver looked up from his work but then continued without noticing them.

"She wants to meet now. The premium version finally paid off. I have to go. Get haircut. Take first bath.

Goodbye," he screamed with delight, climbing up the wall at an inhuman speed.

"No, get back here," the doctor yelled, but it was useless. He was gone.

"Come on." Terra took his arm and said gently, "Before we find him again, you need to learn some manners." The two glided off the ice to be harassed by a security guard who spoke so fast neither one of them understood him.

Nearby, up against the wall in the shadow of one of the skyscrapers, was Horace, who looked unusually glum. As the two approached him, they could hear his phone buzzing every few seconds.

"Dad? Why do you look so down?"

"I sold my soul to the devil once more," he muttered barely above a whisper.

"Frankenstein got away," said the doctor. "I mean the monster. I'm—you know what I mean. Now we'll never find him again."

"That's not true, doctor." Horace's phone buzzed again, and he pulled it out. "I know where he's going. And there isn't an escape route."

"What do you mean?" asked Terra.

"He's going to that skyscraper we used to own. I talked with the new buyer, and he's still turning it into an apartment building, but he'll allow us to go to the twenty-first story."

"But why would that monster be there?" asked the doctor.

"Because that is where he thinks he is going to meet a hot witch for a date," said Horace slowly.

"Dad, you didn't?"

Horace nodded. "I've catfished him."

There was silence for several seconds as Horace's phone buzzed again.

"Apparently, I made a really good account too. I think I've matched with every man on this stupid app."

His phone buzzed again with another poor soul looking for love.

So, it was a dark and stormy night, but to Horace Blackwater, that was just about as normal as a bright and sunny day. A storm had rolled in bringing with it an ominous constant backdrop of thunder as the three approached the skyscraper.

"He just texted me." Horace held up his phone. It had not stopped buzzing the whole way over.

(I apologize for the interruption to this story, however, beta readers found the following passage very disturbing. The things the monster texts Horace and that Horace texts back, in order to remain in his assumed bewitched witch persona, were so cringy that one person threatened a lawsuit. Just imagine a text conversation between two lovers that is so horribly out of touch and you will have imagined something that is not nearly as bad as what was originally written.)

Terra looked as though she would throw up as Horace read the conversation aloud.

The doctor began to chuckle in a stereotypical evil villain laugh as they entered the elevator.

"I think we need to have a different approach this time," said Terra.

Horace frowned. "And you bring this up as we are on the elevator?"

"Well, they just started name-calling each other last time. Maybe we can work out a compromise or something."

"That's very noble of you, Terra," Horace said. "And I'm very proud of you, but I don't think he has any room to negotiate with us now."

The elevator doors opened, and the three saw yet another pitiful sight.

The monster had dressed up in a worn suit, and despite appearing to have had hair last time, now looked like he had a comb-over. His legs were shaking, but his mouth dropped when he saw the three of them.

"What are you three doing here!? I still don't even know who those two are." He pointed at Horace and Terra. "I'll give back your identity if you leave, please, I have an important date, and I don't want you three here."

"That was easy," the doctor mumbled.

"Not quite," Horace said, stepping out of the elevator thrusting his hand high into the sky. "I'm afraid I have some bad news for you."

"Wait, Horace, please, he said he'd give my identity back."

"I have my own goals here, doctor." The elevator door began to close, nearly ruining the dramatic sense of the moment, but Terra caught it, and she and the doctor stepped out as the door tried to close again. "Don't worry, we'll get your identity back."

"My bad news is for you." Horace pulled the brim on his top hat down. "You who call yourself Frankenstein."

"Me!?" Both the monster and doctor said in unison.

"Perhaps I should use a different name then." Horace folded his arms. "My bad news is for…"

(<REDACTED>)

(The redacted word is one of the pet names Horace came up with during their text exchange. Needless to say, in any country without free speech, he would be thrown in jail for coming up with such a string of words.)

The monster's eyes seized, and he began to stumble back. "NO!"

"I'm afraid there is no witch coming to meet you."

"NO! That's impossible!"

"You've been catfished."

"NONONONONONONONO!" the monster repeated as he backed into the wall. He turned around and began to bang on the window which surprisingly withstood each blow.

"You were never loved by an attractive witch! And you

said some very questionable things I now have on my phone."

"Please, no! I just…I wanted…I-I'll do anything just please…" The monster fell to the ground.

"Your love has blinded you, my friend." Horace stepped closer. "And if you want those text conversations and this whole ordeal kept quiet, you will hand back to the doctor the name 'Frankenstein,' and all online information relating to it."

"Yes, it's all yours." The monster collapsed to the ground. "I'll give it all back. I-I'm sorry."

"Yes, score for Frankenstein!" the doctor shouted. He began to dance around… *(badly)*…as the monster continued to sob, and Terra approached her father. She whispered something unheard to either the doctor or the monster.

"Are you sure?" asked Horace.

She nodded. "Please, Dad."

They had come a long way and seen many things. The path a horror agent takes is unique and different for everyone. It's never normal either, but that's not a written rule, it's just one of those implied rules. With Terra's whispered suggestion, Horace knew she would make an excellent agent of horror. One who cared for everyone, and sometimes, like in this case, it might just lead to a better resolution. After all, with the doctor and monster not on speaking terms, the possibility for a sequel was pretty low.

Except for one where the monster got revenge, but well, that would be a little dark.

"Actually," Horace said. The monster looked up from his pool of tears, and the doctor stopped mid-dance. "Well, why don't you tell them, Terra."

Terra smiled and clasped her hands together. "Mr. uh-" It was at this moment she realized the monster still technically didn't have a name. "Mr. Monster Frankenstein, we've decided to delete the conversation, and we won't tell anyone. You don't have to return the identity either."

"R-really?" He sniffled.

"What is this betrayal?" cried the doctor.

Terra turned to the doctor "We won't delete it *if* you agree to share the identity or find one for him since he is your creation."

"What preposterousness is this!?"

Horace put his arm around Terra's shoulder. "You know, Doctor, he's like a son to you in a way. You made him, and you seem to have a lot in common. The least you could do is give him is an honorable identity and a proper name."

The doctor slumped. "Like a son to me? I never thought about it like that." He seemed to be in a serious stupor.

"Father?" The monster said. "I never had one before. What is that like?"

"Oh, it's wonderful when your father is like mine," said Terra.

"And a child?… Well, they can bring you the greatest joy in life," said Horace.

"They can? Even more so than any of my accomplishments could?" asked the doctor.

Horace looked at Terra and smiled. "She makes me happier than any of my achievements," Horace looked down, noticing the little pin on his jacket she had made all those years ago.

The two hugged, and the monster and doctor watched the bond of a family at its best. Each seemed as though they felt a tug in their heart, and maybe longing for something similar.

"Well… uh, would you like to be my father?" the monster asked as a different kind of tear began to come down his face.

"Yes, let's give it a try… Victor Jr."

The monster smiled. "Victor Frankenstein junior."

The doctor grinned. "Of course. I want you to be named after someone you can admire."

The doctor helped the monster to his feet. "You know, if we share the identity, legally we could get a massive tax break."

The monster rubbed his hands together. "We'll be a father and son crime duo."

The two laughed and headed to the elevator.

Horace and Terra had pulled away and waved to see the two off.

"Thanks for everything, Horace," Dr. Frankenstein said.

"Thank you, Terra!" the monster said.

"Oh, but don't do the tax thing!" Horace shouted as the elevator doors closed. "The IRS is no joke!" He wondered if they had heard him.

Regardless, Horace couldn't help but smile. He turned to the window where the storm had parted revealing a beautiful full moon. Such a view required any horror aficionado to take a better look. He stared out the window as his daughter stepped alongside him.

"Did you really mean all that, Dad?" Terra asked with a grin.

Horace put his arm over her shoulder. "Of course I did, dear. And your idea to put them back together was marvelous."

"It wouldn't be right just to side with one," Terra reasoned. "I'm sorry if it got in the way of any plans you had for using one or the other for horror material."

"Ah, don't worry about that. We might still get something out of this, and well,…some things are more important than the next big scare. Not a lot of things are, but occasionally you find something." He looked directly at Terra.

As if on cue, his phone jingled. He pulled it out of his pocket, and his wholesome grin turned cynical.

"Besides," he said ominously. "Did you notice how terrified Victor Jr. looked when he realized he was catfished?"

"So that was always your plan?" Terra's face broke into

her own mischievous grin. "I wondered why you went on with telling him the lie."

"His look was absolutely to die for. I haven't seen anyone so scared since… ever."

"We can use catfishing as the next big scare!"

"Naturally." Horace scrolled through his phone. "And according to my matches, we have nine-hundred and ninety-nine and a plus sign number of beta victims."

"This will truly cement your legacy."

Horace nodded. "I think you mean *our* legacy."

Thus, Horace and Terra Blackwater ushered in a new era of scary attractions and trends. Dating apps would be ruined forever. Horace and Terra were both immortalized and revered in the industry, but most importantly, Horace Blackwater and Terra Blackwater became known as the best father and daughter agents of horror duo. It was a small category, but they were number one!

ABOUT THE AUTHOR

C.J. LAWSON lives in Utah; he was born in Walnut Creek, California, and moved with his family to Utah when he was a teenager. It was there that with a friend and fellow writer, he discovered his passion for writing. He wrote his first novel in eighth grade, and while attending high school he was an active member of the National Speech and Debate Association. Over the years he has received multiple awards and recognitions related to comedic short stories (including one certificate that for some reason, has Elmo on it). He is currently a student again but is holding out hope that this time he will be done with school. He has worked professionally and as a volunteer in several programs helping individuals with autism and Down syndrome.